Dorothy McGuire

A novel

Brian Reddish

Dorothy McGuire
© 2016 Brian Reddish

ISBN 978-0-9934887-1-9

Published by Caracal Books
United Kingdom
www.caracalent.uk

Cover images:
Floral Pattern - www.allfreedownload.com/wedesignhot
Used under creative commons.
Woman: www.shutterstock.com/wrangler
Photo used for illustrative purposes only.

Dedication

This book is dedicated to my three children:
Stephen, Rebecca and Anna.

Foreword

This story focuses much upon the plight of Dorothy McGuire, a most beautiful, intelligent and accomplished young lady, who suffers from the effects of sexual child abuse later on in life. She carries dreadful guilt and shame, blaming herself for not doing enough to stop things in the first place. There is more; whilst she is so beautiful, her innermost being is marred by her low self-esteem and self-worth.

"...the extreme damage deep within her caused by all the hurt from her horrible past - they had the effect of scorching her heart and emotions like a hot iron upon silk...!"

Even so the underlying message of the book points to Dorothy's ardent, determined, and often painstaking pursuit of love and hope through reading the Psalms in her Sunday school Bible. She seeks and searches for help and deliverance or as she puts it:

"...I wish something like this could work to help me! If only God could be that real to me also! If this was written with any purpose at all; if these words are supposed to be relevant for today, they should be able to provide help for me...!"

Dorothy meets a diverse group of friends, in particular, Mary Osborne, a single parent mother with her daughter Julia. The inevitable happens with the accidental appearance of Mary's handsome brother, David Osborne, who challenges Dorothy's feelings and emotions to the limit!

Quite unexpectedly, there emerges substantial religious conflict, triggered by Dorothy's simple childlike faith – and from a source that brings great surprise all-round. Yet it is her newly found wisdom and tenacity that helps point many, young and old alike, towards the saving knowledge and love of God.

From this background develops an unfolding drama! Dorothy's influence and words suddenly bear fruit in surprising ways.

Finally, the scene reaches a climax with Dorothy herself – can she cope with love and romance given her dark past?

Chapter 1

About Dorothy

Dorothy McGuire was by all accounts a most beautiful and elegant lady. A tall, slim figure nicely complemented long, shining chestnut hair that was thick and wavy, hanging well below her narrow chin and curling inwards at the ends.

It has sometimes been said by so called reputable persons that the prerequisite of facial beauty is the possession of wide cheek bones and a pointing chin, in which case Dorothy was well qualified. Her large brown eyes with black, striking, star-like lashes stood out conspicuously. Male onlookers could easily be transfixed if they should gaze at them for more than a few seconds. As facial beauty goes it had to be said that Dorothy was imposing and impressive to almost everyone, except a few whose stare was more like an envious glare! Such was her beauty! Rarely had such extreme reactions been manifested by people in the world as a direct consequence of one person walking through it!

Dorothy was intelligent with a genteel constitution and manner. Born in a rural village in Dorset almost 28 years earlier, she was the only child of a seafaring man who was in the Merchant Navy based in Plymouth. Having had a private education, culminating in her graduation at Oxford, Dorothy now lived secluded and all alone in a one-bedroomed rented flat near Bath. With her qualifications she was able to secure quite a well-paid job in market research.

Given her foundation and start in life and the nature of her curriculum vitae, one would expect a promising future for Dorothy; it would probably be a dream for many, if not all young ladies of her age! However, things are not always what they seem.

Dorothy McGuire had a past – a hurtful past. Her life was not what one could have possibly imagined.

Should it not be normal for such an accomplished and attractive person as Dorothy to experience anything other than happiness and success? Unfortunately, even though she was beautiful, elegant and well qualified those accomplishments alone did not guarantee her a life of joy and bliss!

Whilst so attractive and talented, she had a particular imposition, part of which was reflected in low self-esteem and a low opinion of herself. Her past had done this to her. Any polite compliment or expression of praise attributed to her, especially from a man, was brushed aside with an inward repellent force so that her soul never received the benefits of any such positive consolation.

If one could imagine drops of water trickling down the oily plumage of a duck's feathers and observe how they then roll up into globules so that they do not dampen the feathers, so it was with Dorothy; any compliment accredited to her usually left her untouched and unmoved, just like water off a duck's back!

What had happened to cause this? one might enquire. *Was anything or anyone responsible for her state of mind? Was she hiding a dark past? Was she haunted by an experience from childhood as can sometimes be the case in such situations?*

Certainly, troubled circumstances and situations from childhood can very often have severe repercussions upon people later in life, and therefore can easily be responsible, at least in part, for leaving behind a horribly low opinion of oneself.

The simple answer was yes. Dorothy was such a victim with a dark, traumatic past! She had hurtful childhood experiences with roots that had penetrated very deeply into her personality.

Sadly, such are the experiences of more than a few in a society that has continually progressed in many ways, yet not so in others. Technologically, it has advanced – but morally, ethically or spiritually?

So often now, we hear or read of widespread abuses, whether physical, verbal or otherwise, particularly but not exclusively with children and young people.

Dorothy was the victim of such a plight. She carried wounds from childhood that were not healed. If her troubled state of mind and the burdensome weight of anguish upon her soul could be portrayed in a physical form, one would observe Dorothy carrying heavy loads and baggage upon her shoulders!

Without being too explicit regarding the root cause of her condition at this point in time, it is perhaps sufficient to state that she had suffered sexual abuse from her father as a child and now she tried to live a normal life as best she could. However, plagued by anxiety, guilt, blame, fear and depression, it was an arduous uphill climb each and every day just to survive.

It is said that the most important and essential ingredient to life is the simple compound called water. If the latter is so indispensable for the progress of our health and physical well-being, what remedy could help Dorothy? Her needs were different. No special diet or health program alone could suffice to meet her needs! She forever found the need to keep herself preoccupied – and simply to live and get by – was all too often a burdensome task! Her dark experiences with depression, in particular, would manifest themselves like the giant waves of a cruel sea, oppressing her and flooding over her head, weighing her down!

Oh how she needed an oasis, a place of tranquillity and peace of mind to give her rest! Oh how cruel was the course of time!

Never-ending memories and hurts were endlessly resurgent in her mind and would not die. Escapism and preoccupation facilitated her endurance of the pain for a while, but relapses reared their ugly heads when least expected. No, Dorothy longed for a deeper and more permanent prescription!

———

There were two qualities in particular that could be accredited to Dorothy, underlining and revealing the braveness of her heart and spirit.

First, she had a gentle and humble disposition, and this particular attribute of her character and personality helped her more than she realised by having a significant effect in controlling and calming life's storms that blew in her direction. Rather than succumbing to these onslaughts and being entirely overcome by them, she had devised a therapy whereby she would try to think positively and address her situation by saying to herself that there were many more people far worse off than she.

At least I am fortunate enough to have a nice home and clothes that I like to wear, and I do have a place of work to go to!

In this manner she would try to reassure herself. This was her simple assessment of life when facing difficult moments. By thinking and speaking a positive message over a negative spirit or situation, it helped her challenge, rebuke and neutralise them!

At such times when levels of anxiety became difficult – if not unbearable – she would deliberately try to be constructive and think of something good and enjoyable to occupy her for that moment; she would anticipate something to look forward to. Rather than forever lying down upon her sofa in her sleepy languid posture, she would move herself and make a cup of her favourite camomile tea or read an article in a magazine.

Some instances were less favourable, and the previous strategy was not always successful. The unmerciful onslaughts of mental anguish that plagued her were too much to bear! On such occasions Dorothy would withdraw herself, sit upon the sofa and drift into a staring, pensive state of weeping. Clasping one of her hands in the other as if to provide some comfort and consolation, she would bow her head and shed tears of sorrow.

Dorothy had developed the habit from her school days of tucking a tissue inside the bottom of her sleeve or some other appropriate place. Whenever circumstances were such that she had need of one she would resort to this very place, retrieve the tissue, dab her eyes with it, then place it back again. On some occasions she would get up, walk over to a drawer and replenish her old tissue with a new one.

Though Dorothy was gentle and humble by nature, it did not follow that her temperament and character were weak or fragile. On the contrary, she constantly manifested a determination and zeal to find hope, a hope that would bring her deliverance and provide for the love and care she longed for. This determination was the second quality that could clearly be attributed to Dorothy.

All previous relationships had only left her empty and deluded. Men were understandably attracted to her outwardly, but none had demonstrated the patience and appreciation she needed regarding her inner condition or provided that true and faithful affection that loves you as a person for who you are.

Dorothy was driven by a persistent endeavour to find hope and love. No, Dorothy was not weak; she displayed an outstanding resilience and courage above many of her peers who had no disadvantage such as hers. It was almost as if adversity drew out from within her spirit an inner strength that would have otherwise remained dormant! Nevertheless she suffered! Dorothy suffered!

One evening, Dorothy, having arrived home from work, sat upon a sofa with her favourite drink of camomile tea. She placed her drink upon a nearby table, then laid her head upon a pillow and relaxed.

Now as it happened, Dorothy would sometimes read a Bible she had obtained as a prize from her early childhood attendance at a Sunday school. In particular, she frequently turned to the Book of Psalms, which gave her much comfort. Dorothy loved to read Psalms. To her they often spoke about other people's problems – problems she could relate to. The author was clearly someone who trusted much and had faith and hope, so that in spite of experiencing pain, suffering and reproach, he always seemed to end each Psalm in a positive manner!

This is what I could do with, Dorothy would say to herself in a light-hearted manner. *I wish something like this could work to help me! If only God could be that real to me also! If this was written with any purpose at all… if these words are supposed to be relevant for today, they should be able to provide help for anyone!*

Dorothy clearly had herself in mind with this latter reflection! And so for these reasons she often looked at a Psalm; then she would relax upon her sofa, meditating upon what she had just read.

On this particular evening she slipped into a deep, dreamy sleep having just read Psalm 23 about three times. It had the effect of making her feel quite envious, for even small sheep had a shepherd to love, care and watch over them night and day!

A full hour and a half went by before Dorothy jolted, suddenly waking from her deep sleep. She had had one of those dreams that seemed to be very real with no distinction between sleep and reality, so that upon awakening she was disorientated as to her whereabouts. Then, recollections came back to her, howbeit only temporally. Dorothy had been dreaming quite vividly of frightened sheep running everywhere. She was in a state of panic, anxious with worry, trying to find where the shepherd was to help protect them, but she couldn't find him.

Help me! Where is he?

After this she heard the voice of a person calling out in the far distance while coming towards her, when suddenly there appeared the horrible, frightening face of someone else nearby; it terrified her.

At this point the dream come nightmare ceased. Dorothy awoke quite startled indeed! She sat up and looked around. No sheep! Her dream had been so real and intense, and yet she had been asleep upon a sofa all the time.

She recollected how vivid it had all been – the coolness of the night air, the horrible glaring face of a stranger, and then the voice that had spoken to her in the distance! Recovering her senses she quickly wrote down on paper the details of the dream before it was lost from her memory forever, then placed the paper in her Bible.

That's what you get when you read the Psalms! How odd!

These were her thoughts upon reflection of her dream; she was fairly confident they were connected!

After a while, when Dorothy had calmed herself and was feeling more relaxed, when the awe of her dream had faded, she began to ponder it all, wondering what it could possibly mean. She had read books about dreams and was therefore of a mind to analyse everything.

Reaching for her Bible, Dorothy removed the paper just recently placed there and began reading out aloud the words she had written on it.

A voice had called out to her as if to escape danger. Then there was the hideous face of someone who frightened her and the sheep; they were scattered, running everywhere! Dorothy's first thoughts were that her dream was associated with what she had been reading prior to falling asleep. It was after all about sheep!

She arose nevertheless with some measure of dissatisfaction and frustration and moved towards her bedroom bemused.

Never mind, she thought, attempting to console herself. Then, in an attempt to be released from undue concern regarding the entire experience, she simply said, "It was just a dream!"

It was very late in the evening, and Dorothy was tired as she went into her bedroom. The light in her room stayed on for little more than a minute before it was extinguished. It was the end of an eventful day, and unbeknown to Dorothy this particular day and moment in time would in fact earmark the beginning of a new season in her life!

Chapter 2

Dorothy Goes To Church

Dorothy had a troubled night. Her mind had been so active that she found it difficult to unwind and relax. This was fairly normal for Dorothy. Finding rest and going to sleep did not come easily to her, and since she had already had a nap on the sofa, it was harder still. Eventually, after all her twitching and fidgeting had ceased, she did fall asleep.

She need not have been overly anxious, as her sleep was uninterrupted for at least six hours with no further memorable dreams! Nevertheless, when she did awake and see the light shining through the gap in her curtain, it felt as though she had never slept at all! Getting out of bed while feeling rather sedate and lethargic was an effort for her, but she forced herself to get up and immediately began thinking about what to do that day.

It was always necessary for Dorothy to acquire some purpose in order to occupy her mind, something to look forward to. If she had no real purpose, however trivial, she would enter into a horrible state of depression. The irony was that weekends could be far worse than weekdays, since during the working week there was a fixed routine during the busy day – work! At weekends there was no work and therefore nothing to occupy her! How on earth could she get through the day? What a dreadful state to be in! In the mornings it was always worse. It was the most unimaginable experience ever! Only by going through this state themselves could anyone appreciate and understand just how dreadful this experience was.

It was a Sunday morning. Quite impulsively Dorothy decided what she would do; she would take herself to church! Dorothy was by no means a regular attendee at any church, but on occasions she would visit one. This spontaneous decision was both unprecedented and unpremeditated. Churches were open, and Dorothy needed to be among other people. She could not bear being alone all day!

Perhaps afterwards I could go into town and look around the shops, she thought, *and after that, perhaps go for lunch! This sounds good; my day is planned.*

It had to be said that Dorothy usually found the experience in church rather boring, and the eerie melancholy atmosphere she felt she experienced was not that conducive to helping her state of mind.

In her heart she longed for some consolation for her life, whether spiritual or otherwise, but somehow she always came away in a dissatisfied and disillusioned manner. It was not clear whether or not it was because they never preached on the Psalms at Church or whether it was that she just found it hard to relate the message to her particular need, but the outcome was usually the same.

Today, however, the incentive and aspiration was to go to church, and this is what she was going to do!

By her calculations, Dorothy had a good twenty minutes to prepare herself before it reached 10.30 a.m. It was about that time she had often heard the church bells ringing, waking her up from sleep. Without a thought for having any breakfast, she left the house promptly, there being only a few minutes before the time she supposed the service would begin.

The bells had ceased their ringing, and on arrival at the church door the sound of organ music filled her ears with their greeting and invitation. It was a rather deep and sombre sound that reminded her of a similar occasion in the past when she had needed to turn in her tracks, the music having aroused nervousness within her. The effects were just the same on this occasion; Dorothy instantly stood still as if to avoid a wall directly in front of her.

"Oh!" she exclaimed upon hearing the sound. *I do find this music very sorrowful and sad,* she thought to herself. Rather than wait any further, she simply walked away.

This type of musical sound that was so uninviting to Dorothy may have been quite acceptable and even beautiful to another person! It was not entirely clear why it had such a negative effect upon her ears, but it did, and not having any particular obligation to please the organist, she chose to carry on walking in the same direction as she was going before turning aside to go into the church.

As it happened, Dorothy's face briefly lit up for she had heard about another church not too far away that she could try; it was a fairly new and modern building. However, this particular place did bring reservations to mind because of what she had heard about it. Apparently it was not what you might consider to be a conventional church! Certain elderly ladies, whose comments and opinions were considered above reproach by many in the community, had reiterated in so many words and on more than one occasion that this particular church was most unusual – even though they themselves had never been inside it. The very fact that certain ladies considered it as such implied that it must, therefore, be very odd indeed and consequently could not be good, though the reasoning as to why they inferred it as being odd was not very satisfactory in Dorothy's mind. Dorothy had recollected that the ladies' disapproval was in essence directed at the form and style of worship and various informalities to do with what they considered most inappropriate clothing worn by many who attended the church as opposed to any seriously different doctrinal views. She had been told that there was no organ, but instead young musicians played guitars and drums, and in their opinions, such could not be respectable people in God's House if they wore jeans and tee shirts.

I suppose there were times when wearing such clothes would have been considered inappropriate for church, thought Dorothy. *Back when you only wore jeans to go to work in, that is!*

However, young people would not have been born then, and would therefore be oblivious of such a culture.

In spite of the old ladies' objections, Dorothy was still to be seen walking in the direction of that very same church, seemingly undeterred by the adverse comments and opinions. Perhaps her current mindset was a little more obstinate than usual as a direct result of the ladies' objections, which only had the opposite effect of that intended; they left her even more determined to visit the church!

I have no objection to people wearing jeans if they have a mind to; I do not consider this to be disrespectful, not if they are sincere in their beliefs!

Could it be that the sound of guitars and drums would be more palatable to Dorothy's ears than the recent sound of an organ?

With nervous excitement, Dorothy trotted along quickly in the direction of the forbidden building, knowing full well that what she was about to do would be met with great disapproval by certain people.

Dorothy could see no problem fundamentally with guitars and drums being played in a church either. Her focus was upon receiving that kind of help and consolation she had read about in the Psalms and nothing else! In fact the whole idea of this kind of music was quite different and could be interesting in a church.

She reassured herself by thinking of what she had once read about David. He was a man who had loved God and had written Psalms, yet he had played musical instruments in worship and danced half-naked before the Ark of the Covenant just as it was being brought back to its home in Jerusalem. If God had permitted this of the shepherd boy who became His chosen king over Israel, then it went without saying that it must have also been acceptable to Him!

I don't suppose anyone here will be doing such a thing – dancing before the altar half-naked; that would give the ladies something to talk about!

As Dorothy drew near to the door of the building she observed ahead of her a young couple with two children and a tiny baby just about to enter. The couple turned and greeted Dorothy kindly. Dorothy replied in a similar fashion and thought they seemed friendly enough and appeared quite normal. As a matter of fact, the sight of the children entering the church also helped calm her nerves. She was encouraged by this and assured herself that there was no reason to be afraid of going where they were going!

"Well, let's go in," she said speaking aloud as she approached the door. "Let's see what it is like in here!"

Upon entering the door, Dorothy came into a foyer and could hear music that sounded like guitars and drums. Passing through the foyer, she entered a large hall where the music was significantly louder, sending vibrations reverberating through her body. There must have been at least two to three hundred people all singing and expressing a lively and active sort of worship! She could only describe the scene that met her eyes as extraverted to say the least, the likes of which Dorothy had never seen before! It was more akin to contemporary music, which was in stark contrast to that of the organ she had just cowered away from!

Small children were jumping up and down and moving their arms and bodies to the beat of the music, as were many who were not so young!

Why, thought Dorothy, in part smiling and in part aghast by what met her eyes, *they are dancing! Well, at least no one is half-naked!*

Now she could imagine why the old ladies were so appalled by the church. What had met Dorothy's eyes was not traditional by any means!

The atmosphere and music were contagious, and Dorothy cautiously flowed into the rhythm, releasing just a little of her own enthusiasm and bodily movement – though with some shyness and reserve as she reminded herself that she was actually in a church! Dorothy, trying not to be too conspicuous, peered at the faces of the people around her. While very exuberant and happy, they all seemed normal. She was impressed.

A different form and style of worship to what one is accustomed should not be thought of in a negative manner, if it is sincere and from the heart!

This was Dorothy's growing opinion. Even so, Dorothy did wonder whether or not she had made the right decision to come here and contemplated whether she would be influenced by something that might culminate in regret through naivety. This kind of atmosphere was all new to her.

What if they believe in weird doctrines?

A little anxiety began to manifest itself in her mind, followed by a hot flush, so that she felt it would be more comfortable to move to another seat. Desiring to be inconspicuous and deciding not to leave straight away, Dorothy moved and sat down in the back row.

Dorothy did not usually act as impulsively as she had done that morning in deciding to come to church. She was more accustomed to carefully thinking things through before making a decision about a matter, and would demonstrate a sense of propriety in her manner in a dignified way. However, this was the Dorothy before she had had her dream! Since then she had acquired a somewhat agitated and unsettled frame of mind and was eager to know if coming to church might enlighten her somewhat and perhaps reveal some insight regarding her dream?

Dorothy's opinions and insights were usually profound, but in this respect it was quite the reverse; she was even a little childlike in imagination. She was seeking and searching, rather like a lost sheep; that part of her dream was true!

As the meeting progressed, the music quietened and was replaced with stillness and solemnity. A gentleman, probably in his fifties, and dressed very normally – that is to say with no special religious attire – began to preach.

An observer looking out for newcomers would have noticed a new person sitting alone at the back – a pretty, young lady, smartly dressed, who seemed to be riveted to her seat, leaning slightly forward as if to ensure she heard every word.

Everything that Dorothy had heard from the gentleman thus far seemed quite interesting, inspiring even, and the sort of things she expected to hear in a church. He preached from the Bible as though he believed it! Occasionally the speaker would laugh at some matter, and she found herself laughing too, but then checked herself by placing a hand over her mouth. Dorothy would occasionally turn her head peeking to observe whether others were finding it humorous too.

After all, she thought, *you are not supposed to laugh in church, are you? Or for that matter be particularly happy either! Surely such behaviour in church is disrespectful, is it not? And the elderly ladies would surely agree that everything concerning God must be said and done in a solemn and sober manner!*

This new event for Dorothy, actually sitting in a church meeting, was doing her good! She was totally preoccupied in her mind, and as a consequence, temporarily relieved from any adverse disposition mentally – and it wasn't a weekday either!

The pastor read a passage from John's Gospel, and then began preaching an evangelistic message. Dorothy was listening attentively, when suddenly, his words caught her attention.

"My sheep hear My voice, and I know them, and they follow Me. We all follow something or someone," he said.

Now, the idea of sheep following someone completely gripped Dorothy's attention. Needless to say she had been thinking of her dream with the sheep.

She was spellbound with interest. The pastor's message went on to talk of personal assertions about how God loved each person, and that Jesus died for each one. "Jesus died for you so that you can have a relationship with your Heavenly Father," he said.

Dorothy could not help but smile warmly upon hearing that part. The warmth of heart experienced by Dorothy came about upon hearing the title *father* in the context of one who loved her. This thought, however, was soon replaced and pushed to the back of her mind by a familiar sadness and guilt springing up within her, rather like an unwelcome intrusion into something good.

This was so often Dorothy's plight! Whenever she heard the title *father* spoken, it easily triggered sad repercussions as a direct result of the trauma she had carried mercilessly since childhood, and for which there was seemingly no cure.

To be specific, she had always felt guilty and blamed herself for the things that had happened to her in earlier years. She had constantly blamed herself for not doing enough to prevent them from happening in the first place.

Also, why did I keep it a secret? she asked herself. *Did I encourage the whole abominable thing simply by showing insufficient restraint?* She had always considered herself to blame and felt she should suffer for it!

This was the kind of dreadful condition Dorothy had imagined. It was, of course, completely untrue, unfounded, and from the pit of destruction. But even so, nothing and no one could ever make her feel otherwise!

As she listened and heard it repeatedly said that God her Father loved her personally, one might have noticed a quiver in her lips and a bowing of her head. Yet the preacher continued to reinforce this assertion with relentless passion.

Love would normally bring happiness, but references to the love of her Heavenly Father resurrected unhealed wounds. With Dorothy, the message had the opposite effect to what was intended. The more this phrase was mentioned, the worse she felt. Tears filled her eyes, preceding a bout of continuous sobbing. To remedy this situation, Dorothy, as was her usual custom at such times, placed her right hand inside the sleeve of her left arm, withdrew a hidden tissue, dabbed her eyes with it, and then placed it back again. This moment of tears had not gone unseen, however. Unknown to Dorothy, a certain person happened to have glanced in her direction taking notice of how upset she was.

———————

The meeting finished. People arose and were either withdrawing to the back or standing idly in the aisle talking.

The pastor walked towards the back, stopping to shake hands with various people on his way. Seeing Dorothy, who was a stranger to him, he warmly shook her hand and welcomed her to the church as well.

"It is very nice to see you," he greeted Dorothy, quite oblivious to how she was really feeling. "Welcome!"

Dorothy remained seated in her chair looking down towards the floor. In deep emotional thought, she hardly acknowledged the greeting.

Before too long, a lady also drew close to the place were Dorothy was sitting.

"Hello!" she said in a kindly manner. "How are you? It is nice to see you here!"

The lady asked if Dorothy needed any help, confessing that she had noticed Dorothy's upset during the meeting.

Now, the pastor of the Church, a John Peterson, had a wife called Miriam, a very understanding and kind lady, who was a good twenty years older than Dorothy. It was she who had come over to speak to Dorothy.

Dorothy, still feeling upset and emotional, lifted her head and looked up into the lady's face. Her eyes were puffy and inflamed as they greeted those of Miriam, who sat down next to Dorothy gently placing an arm around her shoulder.

"Can I be of any help or do anything for you?"

Most people had by now left the building so that the two were alone. They talked together for a long time; Miriam listened attentively to what Dorothy had to say. The situation was overdue.

It was needful for Dorothy, at some time or another in her life, to release to the right person those personal things that were pressing upon her – secrets from her past kept hidden for too long. Her pain was seemingly exacerbated by her continually concealing those matters that needed to be shared with someone, and yet the opportunity had never materialised for Dorothy.

Her family, what remained of them, were far too close, and in the past had completely disclaimed any such scandalous notion of a relative of theirs; any accusation or suggestion of abuse from a family member was utterly refuted. Consequently, Dorothy had felt worse for attempting to confide in family members; it brought shame upon shame to her already dismal plight; it contributed more to her blame and guilt! And friends were too embarrassed or uninterested to hear of such things! Who else was there to turn to?

Could Miriam, being an older woman and someone who was totally unknown to Dorothy, be the right person?

Courageously, Dorothy had taken the occasion as an appropriate opportunity to disclose some personal details to her sympathetic and understanding companion.

She initially intended to reveal to Miriam things about her life in a calm and controlled fashion without being particularly melodramatic or emotional, but in the process of trying to do so, she eventually became quite overcome by it all. Dorothy's hurts where very real – the guilt she had endlessly suffered, her shame like leeches from a horrible miry swamp that had clung to her and would not be released. All these distressing memories that had left her in deep depression for what seemed a lifetime could in no way be trivialised, however hard she may have tried. They had released themselves from her innermost being and came up to the surface in the form of tears.

Dorothy could have been likened to a picturesque mountain scene, beautiful in its appearance; yet within its core was a hidden volcano, dormant until its appointed time of eruption – and that designated time for her seemed to be on that particular Sunday morning! The pressures that had accumulated within her, held back and restrained for so long, were to be released!

After a quiet interlude when Dorothy had regained her composure, Miriam sat down to the right of her, and they bowed their heads in prayer. Dorothy was still overcome by tears, and Miriam comforted her by placing her left arm around Dorothy's left shoulder and her right hand upon her right shoulder; she then prayed for the love of God to come upon Dorothy!

Dorothy felt a wave of goose bumps from her head, moving down through her body, followed by warmth that manifested itself and rested upon her. It had the effect of removing all fear, showing her that there was no need to be anxious anymore regarding her Heavenly Father! His presence brought her peace, a sense of security and a personal assurance that He was with her; He was real and aware of everything she was going through! He knew her and would always be there to protect and comfort her!

From that time onwards, Dorothy was no longer afraid of the title *father*, for the predominant memory upon hearing it had now changed from the earthly to that of the Heavenly! This was a moment in time Dorothy would remember forever; something miraculous had happened to her that had changed everything in her mind and heart regarding her very concept of God. In short, she had moved from a theoretical understanding of God to one of a more personal nature!

One moment she was upset – in deep despair, fear and trepidation – but in the next came a warmth and peace that passed all understanding! If Jesus had been standing next to her, it could not have been any more real than it was then!

Dorothy gradually lifted up her head and stared at a verse upon a nearby wall. It read,

Eye has not seen, nor ear heard, nor have entered into the heart of man the things which God has prepared for those who love Him- but God has revealed them to us through His Spirit.

This became one of Dorothy's favourite Scriptures from that time onwards! It always pointed her back to that precious moment in time when God revealed Himself to her by His living presence - the Holy Spirit!

The ladies looked up at each other, and Miriam smiled. Dorothy's countenance, being somewhat restored to normality, was peaceful, and she looked happier. Her cheeks were quite flushed, but there was a warm glow about them, and a twinkle of light in her eyes manifested a radiance that suggested the worst was over!

Having revealed to Miriam something of her past sufferings as a child and having disclosed how she had been hurt and abused by her father for many years, she entered into a state of calm and great relief that was most welcome.

Both of them stood and gave one another a hug. *Could there be any truth in the saying: a problem shared is a problem halved?* wondered Dorothy.

Before departing, they each wrote something down on paper and passed it to one other.

"I am pleased you came this morning, Dorothy," said Miriam. "You have been extremely brave and have done a very wonderful thing today! God will watch over you, and He has promised never to leave you or forsake you! I hope we can meet up again if you so wish. Take care, and God bless you! I will think of you and pray for you."

Dorothy replied with a simple 'thank you' and they went their separate ways.

____

Now as it happened, there was a certain young lady still in the church building who, having stayed behind with some of the band of musicians, happened to look up as Dorothy was leaving and straightway moved briskly in her direction to catch her attention before she left.

"Hello, my name is Maria. I have not seen you before. Is this your first visit?"

The girl must have been no more than sixteen or seventeen years of age. She was clearly very happy to see another young lady in church.

"Hello. My name is Dorothy, and yes... it is my first visit," she replied. Dorothy was pleasantly surprised by Maria's simple warmth, smiles and friendliness.

"My, you are very pretty!" said Maria unreservedly. Maria was a typical young lady, whose thoughts, words and feelings were close to the surface. What came from her lips came from her heart; simple outspokenness was very normal for her generation, but it tended not to be so from those outside of it.

"Thank you," replied Dorothy.

Continuing with her frankness, Maria asked in her natural uninhibited manner, "And will you come again?"

Dorothy surprisingly felt very comfortable with the conversation in spite of Maria's directness. It was light, innocent and quite a refreshing change for Dorothy to hear a person get straight to the point in the manner shown by Maria.

"Well, thank you. I'm not sure just yet. I have a few things to think about first, but I may well do so," said Dorothy. "I do like the music very much. Are you the young lady who was singing in the band on the stage?"

"Yes," smiled Maria. "Oh, please come again, Dorothy! I would love to chat with you about things. Oh, please come; it would be like awesome if you did!"

Dorothy, again surprised by Maria's persistence and directness, assured her that she would certainly hope to come the following Sunday.

"See you on Sunday, Dorothy!" Maria was very excited by her success and so pleased with her new contact that she gave Dorothy a spontaneous hug, and then left.

Chapter 3

A Surprise Meeting in Town

It was 9.30 a.m. on Monday morning. Dorothy had just finished breakfast and was relaxing upon the sofa, her mind quite positive and well for a change, as mornings in particular could be a difficult time.

Sipping her tea she stared through her window at the blue sky and green trees, musing about what had happened the previous day – her decision to give her heart to the Lord, her conversation with Miriam, and the sense of peace and warmth of God's love experienced as never before. She had felt as though God had actually come to her as she was sitting there in church with Miriam close by her side. What an encounter! It had been real. Something she would never forget. Never before had she known such an experience as this; she had imprinted upon her soul forever that God is real!

Why I feel quite a new person, she thought, *like there is a great load off of my mind!*

It was her day off work, and Dorothy, having finished her tea, took her jacket and trotted down the stairs to go out, intending to catch a bus and go into town. The front door was ajar, and an elderly man called George, the downstairs tenant, was busy working on the small patch of front garden. Seeing Dorothy, he said, "Good morning to you, Dorothy; just going out?"

"Good morning, George. Yes, I thought of going down town for a while. It's my day off work."

"You look very happy if I may say so," declared George in a sort of uninhibited forward manner, quite normal with those who are over the age of sixty-five years and sometimes embarrassing to those who are not. George went on further to say, "Reckon you must be in love!"

Dorothy glared at him with shock, "Do you think so, George?"

"What! Do I think you must be in love?"

"No, but what you said before that. Do you really think I look happy?"

"Why, you look as bright and sharp as a fresh spark off a grinder! Yes, you look happy to me, dear child, and very lovely as usual."

"Well, thank you for that," retorted Dorothy, her sheepish smirk becoming a half smile. "See you later!"

Poor George scratched his head, replaying the conversation that had just taken place, and thought to himself that he still had a long way to go regarding his understanding of modern young ladies.

However, he would never know the wonderful effect his greeting had had upon Dorothy, for it was the first time she had ever been told she looked happy – no, very happy!

Dorothy had caught a bus fairly quickly and was now walking down the high street in town, browsing through the occasional shop or two. Window shopping had always been good therapy. She browsed the latest fashions, knick-knacks – otherwise known as dust collectors, household goods, bedding and any other things such as are found in shops in a busy town.

Occasionally, Dorothy would instinctively wander into baby shops and gaze at the beautiful outfits which seemed so full of colour these days. Dreams of ever needing to buy such goods seemed so remote, but that did not stop her heart from wishful thinking. Most of the shopping area was pedestrianised and therefore spacious and suitable for casual, stress-free walking about.

What else do you do on your day off work? she thought.

It was during this preoccupation of her time that Dorothy heard a loud voice addressing her by name. Turning aside, who should she see in front of her, but Maria!

"Hi, Dorothy, Fancy seeing you here!"

"Hello, Maria! We meet again!"

It seemed these two young ladies did not require much time to get to know one another in order to warrant a warm hug, for instantly upon meeting they embraced affectionately.

"Oh! It's just so great to see you again, Dorothy. Are you busy or doing anything special?" Maria asked.

"No, not really, Maria… just strolling around window shopping. It is such a lovely, warm day; I felt like coming out."

"Yeah, so did I, I needed to get out of the house actually. Should we go somewhere and sit down?"

"How about a coffee?" replied Dorothy.

"Yeah, great. Let's go in here," said Maria with great excitement, pointing to the nearest coffee shop – one of several in the locality.

Now, Maria had wanted to get out of her house, as she put it, for a specific reason, and Dorothy went on to ask her if all was well at home. Maria looked Dorothy in the eyes as if checking her out, wondering whether to talk about personal specifics or not. But then, having weighed Dorothy up as a nice person with whom she felt safe, she easily moved into her usual free manner of speaking.

"Oh, it was my dad again! He had a bad night last night."

"Oh dear, sorry to hear; what exactly was the trouble?" enquired Dorothy with genuine earnestness.

"Oh, Dorothy, you don't want to know!" she exclaimed, but then intending to continue anyway went on to say, "He came home drunk again and was angry – with himself mostly, but also with my mum who had popped round to see me as she sometimes does. It really does upset me you know! I just had to get out of the house this morning, out of the way; they kept on arguing, so I came straight here and met up with you! He's a nutter when he's like that!"

"Oh, Maria, that's terrible! How long has he been this way?"

"Oh, about six months I suppose. He started going to the hospital about two weeks ago, and goes in once a week for some sort of treatment... but when he starts to come off of the drink, that's when the real trouble starts. He gets irritable with everyone over the slightest thing. Like if you are just doing normal things, you know, like playing music or something and making a little noise... that's when he can go ballistic! I turn my music down, but it makes no difference – not when he has a bee in his bonnet! Other times he looks really pale and ill with like a fever, and I feel sorry for him. Anyway, we are all praying for him at church... that he will get better."

Upon hearing the latter remark, Dorothy noticed a teardrop on Maria's cheek as she became momentarily silent, but then she rubbed it away quickly wanting to hide all appearance of being upset. Dorothy, taken somewhat by surprise with these revelations regarding Maria's father, really wondered just what to say in response. She had never been in such a situation before – actually listening to explicit descriptions about one who could only be described as an alcoholic and how it affected a young family member, someone who was in fact sitting right opposite her! This was a live situation, and Dorothy could only search her own heart as to what she would say next that would possibly be helpful to Maria.

Oh, what pains go on behind closed doors! thought Dorothy. *Poor Maria, having to face such a dilemma in her own home – and with her own father! It should not be possible in a modern advanced age for such atrocities as this to happen- but it is!*

Maria is only seventeen. Her father is an alcoholic. Her mother has left home. She's engaged, like the majority of young people her age, with a college course of study for her future. But under these circumstances and bearing these inflictions upon her young person, she finds herself having to cope with all of this baggage at home – none of which is of her own doing! Thank God she prays and loves the Lord!

My own problematic and long term situation is by the way; I have great compassion towards Maria. I desire with all my heart to help her in whatever way possible.

These had been Dorothy's thoughts and the movings upon her heart for Maria and her plight. She decided the best and only option at the moment was to speak simply and just as freely as Maria had in expounding her own feelings. "Maria, let me help in any way I possibly can. Thank you for telling me about your father. I am here for you anytime. I also will pray for you and your father."

Maria looked up at Dorothy and smiled at her warmly and affectionately, for she had been bowed down momentarily, simply staring at the table in deep thought.

Could Dorothy be a real friend to me? Maria wondered. *Someone with whom I can share matters regarding my private life if necessary?*

The thought of Dorothy praying for her dad had particularly touched her.

Having observed Maria's positive reaction to her offer of friendship and help, Dorothy reached her hand across the table, placed it upon Maria's, and said, "Maria, you and I will help each other, right? Is that agreed?"

"You bet," replied Maria. "But in what way can I possibly be of help to you, Dorothy?"

"You will be surprised, Maria! In fact you have already helped me quite a lot, for I have completely forgotten about myself this last half an hour and have thought only of you."

It was not anticipated by Maria at that particular moment in time just what was to follow next; as they both stood up to leave, Dorothy spontaneously went over to embrace her friend warmly – and with rising compassion and affection! Maria's eyes suddenly watered; Dorothy kissed her cheek, and off they went back to the real world again.

It had been a Divine meeting for the two of them that day. God was on Maria's case in the person of His angel called Dorothy!

Chapter 4

Miriam's Letter

Five days had elapsed since that Sunday morning in Church, and with it being a Friday evening, Dorothy was just entering her front door after a week at work. As was her habit, she picked up the mail, made her way to the kitchen, and prepared herself a cup of her usual tea.

There was always a sense of accomplishment and fulfilment for Dorothy whenever it reached the end of the week. She felt satisfied and pleased with herself for having gone to work each day and having done what was required of her. Every day could be a challenge and a strain for her to get through. This was normal. Now, with the weekend ahead, she looked forward to seeing Miriam and Maria, her newly found friend, again on Sunday.

Glancing through the mail with one hand and sipping her tea with the other, Dorothy observed that one of her letters displayed unfamiliar handwriting. She opened the envelope excitedly and read as follows:

Dear Dorothy

I was so pleased to talk with you last Sunday. You are a most wonderful person, Dorothy, and I was very sorry to hear what you had to say when you kindly

Upon reading Miriam's letter, Dorothy went to get her Bible to read about the Sunday morning sermon that had so interested her. Rushing to her bedroom she saw that it was not lying in the usual place upon the bedside cabinet. "Oh!" she exclaimed. "I must have left it upon my desk at work! I will have to wait until tomorrow now before I can read it!"

Many staff went into work over the weekend, especially when having the pressure of meeting set targets with specific deadlines. Dorothy had already decided she would go into work on the morrow and collect it.

The evening drew on, and having made herself a meal, Dorothy was now seated upon the sofa, relaxing and meditating upon recent happenings and the changes that had come into her life. So much had taken place in less than one week! The dream, the church meeting, her new friendships with Miriam and with Maria!

Then there was the wonderful experience of release she had known with Miriam as they talked and prayed together. It had been a great relief to share with someone else things about herself. As a consequence her interest in such matters had increased. She had discovered and experienced a tangible love and comfort! It was so reassuring! Dorothy couldn't remember the last time she had felt so good and happy.

Words that she had heard on Sunday morning kept going through her mind.

The Good Shepherd watched over his sheep; people represented as sheep and each one known and cared for; the shepherd calling his sheep by name and being followed by them!

Dorothy was intrigued by all of this and couldn't help pondering her dream again, trying to find any possible meaning in relation to her own situation, quite in spite of Miriam's apparent reservations as disclosed in her letter. If what she had experienced that night in her sleep was relevant to her as a person, then she craved more understanding and enlightenment. If it were simply a dream or a nightmare, then she could forget about it. The uncertainty was irritating. However, whatever the outcome, she did understand one thing; just as sheep know their shepherd and follow him, likewise, any person could follow God, whom the pastor likened to the Good Shepherd!

"This also includes me! *Anyone* means I am included!" Dorothy asserted.

Dorothy spent the rest of the evening thinking and meditating on what she had previously read in her Bible. It had become so very real to her, and meaningful. She had on one occasion decided to look up the word *dreams* in her concordance and had come up with several verses that related to God speaking to people through dreams. One example she read about was in the Christmas story. God had warned the wise men in a dream not to go back to Herod to inform him that they had found the Christ, but to depart into their own country another way.

Dorothy cautiously concluded that the assumption that any particular dream was from such a source was not the wisest interpretation to make, only that they can sometimes be of that origin. However, it was still Dorothy's conviction that she might have received such a dream! The thought of being spoken to directly gave her a buzz. Though it was all mixed up as dreams often are, could it still have been possible that God was seeking to speak to her about coming to Him and receiving Jesus as her Saviour? All that she had heard in church confirmed this in her reckoning. Whether or not Dorothy's dream was important or irrelevant, one thing was sure, she did have a real experience that morning in church. The Word she received, as well as the counsel of Miriam, was wonderfully helpful, bringing her great blessing and a sense of liberty and freedom never experienced before.

Now, Miriam had shown her a verse that said:

As many as received Him, to them He gave the right to become children of God, even to them which believe on His Name.

Dorothy had responded to this invite just as it was written. It was very simple; Jesus had made it possible for anyone to come to God through Him. She believed this and all that He had done for her on the cross, and that it was necessary to turn aside from her old life and way of thinking and receive a new life in Christ. The basis of everything was God's grace and His great love for each one who comes to Him through His Son!

Dorothy had considered this as something possible to pursue, with no strain or painstaking effort and with nothing to lose, only to gain!

To Dorothy, this heralded a new enthusiasm in her life. Perhaps she could build herself up and hopefully get her life back together again with new hope and purpose, both of which had been sadly missing until now.

Dorothy did not know what the future held, but whatever she had to endure in overcoming her condition and state of mind, she felt she could now share things with her new friends and not be alone. To be able to trust in someone else would help; to have a hope through believing in God's love would be a source of resilience and strength not solely based upon her own efforts, but upon the work of another outside of herself.

Dorothy had once read that this was supported by certain professionals as a possible therapy for some who had faith in God; it did help! If it did work for Dorothy, she might just be diverted enough from the terrible – even suicidal – aspects of manic depression that haunted her.

Yes, things are finally, howbeit slowly, going to improve, thought Dorothy. There was not a quick solution regarding these matters, but she saw a new glimmer of light at the end of the tunnel now! At long last there was something outside of herself to live for! Her disorder, being typical of so many who also experience its dreadful oppression, appeared to be now under attack by almighty and powerful allies – faith, love and friendship! It was rather like the positive doing battle against the negative. With Miriam's advice, she had wisely decided to continue taking medication to help her from day to day, and this strategy, together with everything else, gave a sense of belonging and stability to her life like never before.

It had been a great struggle for Dorothy with her condition up until now, especially regarding the taking of medication. One of the greatest enemies of her condition and well-being had been the lack of understanding from other people who would often say to her, "Can't you just shrug out of this, my dear, and pull yourself together?"

Others had commented negatively, "Now, you don't wish to go down that road, Dorothy; do you?"

As a consequence, she had refrained from taking medication in the past because of such adverse comments and the stigma that came with them, making her feel guilty if she ever pursued such a route. It was a dilemma, the effects of which made her feel a sense of defeat through having to resort to taking tablets; like a sign of weakness. Had she suffered from any other sickness, it would have been just fine to take prescribed medication! As a consequence, when dark moments occurred – and they often did – she only felt guilty for not being able to cope, for not having the strength to shrug it all off! Oh! The unnecessary, hurtful stigma and sense of failure and condemnation this imposed!

Now, thanks to Miriam's encouragement, the thought of actually taking medication for her sickness was a positive thing to her. It made her feel she was doing something to help herself leaving her with the hope that things should eventually get better. Life had been difficult for Dorothy, but at least now she was starting to move forward on a new path never trodden before.

She was brave and determined and what transpired out of all this was a burning desire in Dorothy to help and inspire others to overcome their hurts and problems, too, just as she was doing! Out of her own difficulties and experiences was born in Dorothy's heart a desire to help those who suffered in a similar fashion to herself! From her own troubles was born a positive remedy of understanding and empathy, love and compassion.

Could this turnaround be more of wishful thinking? Was this all too fast a change? Problems do not always go so quickly in reality. They take time. There are relapses that are inevitable. Whatever the analysis to be made concerning the brutal realities of life, Dorothy was undeterred at this moment in time. Such ups and downs had always been the norm for

Dorothy in the past anyway. It would be nothing new if some still reoccurred from time to time!

Chapter 5

Dorothy Goes to her Office

The following morning could not have come quickly enough. It was a Saturday. Dorothy had gotten out of bed with a new sense of vigour and exhilaration.

Her usual bad feeling, normally felt at this time of day, seemed to have disappeared – at least on this particular morning. Something was now impending for her to do which was most exciting!

It was not very long before she was dressed and walking out of her front door.

There was a fine but appreciable drizzle of rain in the air, and Dorothy had dressed accordingly. She wore a brown leather coat reaching just above the knee. Her tall boots were a matching brown and were tightly laced and fitted to her legs to a few inches below her knee. In her hand was a petite, lighter brown umbrella which was barely sufficient for its purpose. This attire housed the elegant Dorothy as she trotted down the street, holding her opened umbrella as close as possible above her head.

In Dorothy's mind, it was imperative to keep up her good appearance, even if she felt terrible! In fact, this frame of mind and the attitude that Dorothy held towards her appearance was far from any egoistic self-loving aspiration that one might have. It was rather like one simple aspect of a therapeutic remedy and package that promoted her sense of well-being by helping to build her self-esteem and confidence. Just for a moment, just for a time, she felt good and had no problems. She would enjoy looking good and feeling good by going out.

Dorothy had to visit a particular place that morning. She must have walked for twenty minutes or so, when she turned, having reached her destination, and walked towards a tall building. Placing her hand in a pocket, she withdrew a key and opened a door; then, scurrying down a corridor, she came to a lift and summoned it. Upon reaching the seventh floor, she left the lift and hurried through another door, which led to a small open-plan office. Moving to a nearby desk facing a window, Dorothy was relieved to see a large book left open on the desk. It was the Bible she had forgotten to bring home from work the previous day, and it lay open at a Psalm were Dorothy had left off reading.

She went and sat down at her desk and withdrew from her handbag the letter that Miriam had sent her during the week and read it over again.

It was so nice to receive a letter that had been written by hand and not a text or e-mail!

Staring out the window, she drifted off into thought.

Dorothy recollected once again all that had happened to her recently. It was continuously predominant in her mind and would not go away! Everything seemed too good to be true! Now, she could not imagine what it would be like living without the new life she had recently received. The mere thought of her previous loneliness and isolation was just too awful to even think about. The transforming effect of recent happenings responsible for the positive changes to Dorothy's life was bringing the love and comfort of which she had been so desperately deprived in the past.

It had not occurred to Dorothy before now how that, on the night before her dream, her heart had been calling for help after reading and thinking about her Psalm!

Yes, I was very upset at the time and feeling quite low, she recollected. *I remember saying, 'I could do with some of this!' Well, maybe my prayer was heard and answered after all! Perhaps my mixed-up dream really did have elements, at least in part, which were a sort of confirmation that I had been heard.*

The thought of any Divine revelation or guidance had kept running through Dorothy's mind! It was not something difficult or ominous for her to cope with given her disposition. No, Dorothy reacted positively to the whole concept and asserted to herself thoughtfully, *I feel very special and blessed! How wonderful this is!*

Dorothy's heart was young, vibrant, and very excitable at this time of her life. New things were happening to her, with a hint of mystery and imagination, and she relished them all! She placed her hands upon the Bible as it lay open before her, then she bowed her head and prayed aloud, a simple prayer with a grateful and thankful heart.

"Thank you, Lord. Thank you for what you are doing in my life. Thank you, heavenly Father, for your great love towards me!"

Dorothy sat at her desk for quite a long while and recalled the moment last Sunday in church when Miriam had cautioned her quite formally and soberly regarding her dream and had advised her not to take dreams that seriously. 'Unless they are in agreement with the Word of God,' she had said. 'And God's will. Miriam had advised that this was a good and sound approach to these things.

Undeterred by this recollection, Dorothy sat back in her chair. Her face was flushed and glowed with a beaming smile; then, with her eyes closed again, she prayed, "Lord, help me to help others in the same way you are helping me."

This love and compassion had been birthed deep within her heart. Her response to every experience and encounter with her God thus far was simply this: to reach out to others as He, in His Love and mercy, had reached out to her!

Dorothy suddenly thought about the time. It was getting late, and there was something else she wanted to do. There was a certain person she longed to speak to and had many questions for.

After making a phone call, Dorothy left the office and went on her way to visit her new friend, Miriam.

Chapter 6

Dorothy Shows Kindness to a Stranger

Miriam had woken up rather late that morning and had just been thinking of making herself a cup of tea prior to receiving Dorothy's phone call, so now she placed two cups and saucers upon the table instead of one.

The doorbell rang. They embraced each other warmly at the door, and Miriam gave Dorothy a kiss upon her cheek.

"What a lovely leather coat, Dorothy!" greeted Miriam. "Let me take it and hang it up for you."

Dorothy replied to the effect that her coat was indeed nice, but the prevalent thoughts upon her mind were more preoccupying than that of a fashionable coat, and she hardly took notice of Miriam's compliment. And so the two ladies sat down together and conversed attentively. Dorothy began by re-iterating to Miriam how she had left her Bible at work and had returned to get it, that she was feeling so much better now than before, and thanked her for her letter. She told Miriam how she had met up with Maria in town and had a very meaningful conversation with her, though the specific details regarding Maria's father were left out.

They talked together for a period of not less than one hour when Miriam, upon hearing all that Dorothy had to say and being herself also overawed and ecstatic with Dorothy's enthusiasm, posed the following question, "So how do you feel about all of this, Dorothy?"

The question was deliberately asked in a sort of practical but searching fashion to see how she would respond, for so often, when the music of life's excitement fades and the less exhilarating quietness of normality appears all too quickly, it is then that things can change and resort back to a previous state. What would she be left with after the fervour had all passed? A memory that was soon to be forgotten? A bubble now burst being replaced instead by disappointment and despondency? And all because of false or unrealistic expectations leaving her disillusioned and empty! Miriam's concern for Dorothy was tomorrow's life and journey and not just today's elations that all too soon become past experiences contributing nothing more to life. Yes, she rejoiced with Dorothy, but how would she address every day realities and the normal routines of her life when the excitement of her dreams and revelations had ceased? How would this affect Dorothy's life and delicate condition? What would she do with herself?

"How do I feel?" replied Dorothy confidently. "I feel very good, but I would like to help others in a similar state of mind in the way I have been helped. I wish to bless other people!" she declared in a sincere and serious manner with seemingly deep conviction.

"God bless you then, Dorothy, and may you be given the strength and perseverance of heart and mind to pursue this endeavour through thick and thin and do just as you have spoken!"

After a little prayer together, they decided it would be good to go out shopping and have a coffee. The rain had stopped, and there was a glimmer of sunshine between broken clouds.

Very soon they were walking down the high street together, tracing the very same steps Dorothy had walked with Maria on a previous occasion. Both were attentive to certain shop window fronts most applicable and relevant to those ladies with a keen eye for fashion.

Just ahead of them was a department store with prominent sale signs displayed.

"Mm," said Miriam, "shall we take a look?"

"Well, if you insist," replied Dorothy with a cheeky smile, and so they both entered the store, each displaying a gleeful countenance. Miriam immediately noticed a purple top on display in the window.

"Ah! This would suit you fine!" exclaimed Miriam. Nevertheless, they carried on inside and scrutinised every rack and observed all the

different designs before them, but to no avail;
they finally resorted to the purple top first seen
in the window! Miriam insisted Dorothy should
try it on.

"That looks lovely on you," commented
Miriam as she observed the figure of Dorothy
wearing the long, woolly, purple top. Her
appearance was not unlike the mannequin in the
window; she was just as slim, tall and elegant in
it! Miriam added further praise.

"Why, it was made for you!" she retorted
happily. And so it was that Dorothy became the
owner of a new purple top that day!

Now it was time, thought Miriam, to take
Dorothy to her favourite café for a drink, so they
went together in perfect unity and agreement.
Any onlookers observing the pair as they
walked together in unison, smiling and
conversing so heartily with one another, would
perhaps have mistakenly imagined that they had
known each other for years instead of just a
mere few days!

They soon reached the café of Miriam's
choice, a place called *Max's*. Upon entering,
Dorothy saw a large round table just to the right
of the door which was empty and insisted that
Miriam be seated whilst she ordered two lattés.

Shortly, Dorothy returned with the
drinks. As they conversed together, relaxing and
enjoying the leisurely atmosphere and ambience
of the room, a lady happened to enter the café

and walk over to the counter. She ordered a drink and was about to pay for it, when it became apparent that she had insufficient money to do so and turned away to leave, her embarrassment being quite visible to an observant person.

At this point, Dorothy, who had noticed everything, stood up and approached the lady before she reached the door and invited her to join them at their table for a coffee. The lady looked into Dorothy's eyes for a moment curious to have been approached in such a way by a complete stranger. She was visibly shaken at the invitation, but her countenance expressed more than that. Her eyes were heavy and darkened with strain and tiredness; they were perplexed and embarrassed.

The lady thought to herself, *Why would such a person as this elegant and beautiful lady approach the likes of me?*

She felt conspicuous and afraid, but Dorothy, immediately sensing her embarrassment and intimidation, responded and spoke in a warm, friendly manner to diffuse the situation.

"Oh! Please come and join us! We have just been shopping, and I've bought myself a top. Come and see."

This display of kindness on Dorothy's part enabled the lady to feel more comfortable, and so she obliged and walked with Dorothy towards the round table where Miriam was sitting.

Dorothy ordered the coffee of her choice and persuaded her to choose a cake or pastry to go with it. Miriam was impressed by Dorothy's friendly manner and the compassion and generosity she had just shown. She observed Dorothy intently, but discreetly, as she chatted unreservedly to her new friend and heard her talk quite openly and freely about her long prevailing condition and how she had recently found such wonderful help. This frankness and honesty on Dorothy's part provoked in her friend a similar freedom to speak openly about herself too, as if pleased and relieved to talk to someone who could empathise with her and understand her difficulties as well.

Miriam, sitting back in her chair, gazed in awe at the shining face of Dorothy as if observing the face of an angel and thought to herself, *I do believe God has called this person for a purpose!*

Chapter 7

The Guest Speaker

Three months had elapsed since Dorothy McGuire and Miriam Peterson had sat together drinking coffee at *Max's*.

It was a Sunday evening. The church hall, where Dorothy had first entered nervously and apprehensively, was becoming quite full. Ushers were busily directing and escorting visitors to appropriate seats. So often, in such cases, people preferring to sit nearer the back would have to be directed elsewhere nearer the front, because those rows were already taken, but in this case it was quite the reverse. The front rows were either taken or reserved, and people were forced to sit in the middle or at the back!

Soft music was being played in the background, filling the room with a relaxing atmosphere. Some musicians took their positions on the stage and began plucking strings repetitively on their guitars, fine-tuning them. A keyboard musician had very little to do to his musical instrument but plug it in and play a chord or two. He would briefly play a few notes for the benefit of the guitarists, so that they could ensure they were tuned to his keyboard.

Some young ladies stood on the stage area checking their microphones to see if they were working to their satisfaction. One muttered the words 'one-two,' whilst another preferred to gently tap the mike; the outcome in both cases seemed to satisfy them that all was ready.

Fairly soon, Miriam came onto the stage. She was, in fact, convening the meeting that particular night and welcomed all who had come to the church. She summarised the events of the evening, culminating in the announcement that there was to be a special guest speaker.

Afterwards, the musicians played, the band sang, and a rapturous sound of singing, praise and worship ensued. The atmosphere was electric, charged with a sort of joyous flowing energy that filled the room. The music, the beat, the singing, the rapturous response from the people gathered together in the hall that night – all produced a message to any newcomer that this was going to be a dynamic if not energetic meeting. It created a great sense of excitement and expectancy to whatever was going to follow.

After several songs, Miriam stepped back onto the stage. She ventured towards the microphone to introduce the guest speaker. There was a pause; the room hushed with silent expectancy, and then Miriam announced her guest, "Please welcome, Dorothy McGuire!"

Dorothy, who had once entered the same church with curiosity and who had sat nervously at the rear of the building, now came forward on this occasion onto the stage itself smiling and waving to the congregation, which seemed more than pleased to see her in this new role. Not the least was a certain young lady called Maria who was particularly ecstatic in welcoming her friend, Dorothy. She was the girl who, on Dorothy's very first visit, had sought to invite her again to the church and who had since become a great friend, one with whom she could confide. Clearly Maria's wish had come into fruition, for she was now standing up and clapping vigorously to welcome her friend, making certain audible appreciations as well!

"It is my privilege and honour to be asked to speak to you this evening," began Dorothy, "and I only hope that what I have to say will be of encouragement and blessing to all of you, in particular, all you ladies!" This latter part of her intro was welcomed rapturously.

Dorothy spoke with confidence and liberty to the large gathering before her, which consisted of many young people – especially young ladies. She began to describe some of her personal experiences as a young girl, how she had felt unloved and insecure for many years having suffered abuse that led to severe depression later in life. She grew up with a low self-esteem, a negative outlook in life, and a strong sense of personal guilt and shame, certain that she was somehow to blame for every adverse thing that had happened to her.

"I wish to talk this evening about a matter that has helped me a lot of late. Our attitude and manner of thinking can be so negative. For example, a friend of mine at work had had so many broken relationships. She was in despair, and as a consequence often spoke negatively about herself saying things such as, 'I am hopeless and all alone. No one loves me!'

"Of late, I have come to realise that such assertions are not entirely true or edifying, especially for a Christian, since you know there is One Who loves you, and you don't have to feel all alone!

"Later on, the same lady was challenged by this, and instead of all her negative rhetoric, she began to speak quite differently about herself. For example, she would now say, 'I have had many disappointments with relationships, but God still loves me! He has promised that He will never leave me, nor forsake me. I believe He is in charge of my future, and if I choose to put Him first in my life, He will make a way for me,' ... or words to this effect!"

Dorothy continued, "Why not say something like this to yourself every time you get up in the morning? 'I am special. I am loved. He will never give up on me. I have a purpose and a future!'"

After much exposition, it was clear that Dorothy's ministry was having some effect. The whole congregation seemed to utter approval as if to say, 'Yes! This is what we need to hear!'

The fact that Dorothy had previously experienced so much hurt and negativity in her own life merely endorsed and authenticated all she had said. She was not just talking theoretically but had experienced first-hand everything she was telling the congregation. It was this kind of authentic testimony that was indisputable and carried so much more weight than the usual message preached in a church. The Word of God was integrated within Dorothy's real life situations and predicaments. People could relate to it and very easily appropriate it for themselves.

The meeting finished, and Dorothy received many warm greetings of encouragement and thanks.

"Nice one, Dorothy!" exclaimed Ian who was the drummer.

"That was awesome!" said Maria, the lead singer.

Dorothy smiled and thanked them for their approval, and then she sat down on the front row for a while with Miriam.

One more opportunity was provided for Ian to hit the drums and for Maria to sing along with the band for the final song, after which John closed the meeting in prayer and people slowly began to leave.

As Dorothy herself walked towards the door of the hall to leave, a certain young gentleman cut across her path and came over to speak to her. He was a handsome man dressed smartly in a suit and probably just a little older than Dorothy. Speaking with a gentle, polite manner, he said to Dorothy, "Thank you, Miss McGuire, for your words and ministry this evening; I found them quite interesting. It has been a pleasure to have heard you tonight."

"That's quite alright," smiled Dorothy as she turned to look towards him. Her face, as if burning with fire had already been blossoming with an exhilarating radiance as a direct consequence of the excitement of the meeting and it appeared to blossom slightly more upon hearing herself addressed as *Miss McGuire* by such a smart, handsome gentleman!

She had ministered to the congregation with great emotion that evening, as well as with sincere conviction, the effects of which had left Dorothy feeling accomplished and well-pleased with herself.

Dorothy eyes locked briefly with those of the gentleman. She was particularly taken aback by his manner of speech which was wrapped in a warmness of complete respect. Being influenced by his genteel mannerism, she reciprocated in similitude with a quiet placidness by lowering her own voice.

"Thank you; it has been my pleasure."

Rarely, it had to be said, was Dorothy ever moved within herself or made to feel self-conscious in any way, shape or form by the presence of a young man as she was at this particular moment in time! On the contrary, such a situation as this would usually have had the detrimental effect of freezing her up of all conversation and stifling her of any of the normal emotional feelings a young lady might sometimes have felt towards a member of the opposite sex. This tragic frame of mind of hers had most likely been derived as an offshoot from her childhood traumas, from the extreme damage deep within her caused by all the hurt from her horrible past. They had the effect of scorching her heart and emotions like a hot iron upon silk!

What was it then that had brought about this rare change in Dorothy as she stood in this particular gentleman's presence, conversing with him about the recent events that had taken place in a church meeting? Whatever the reason, the amazing fact was that it was real; it was actually happening to Dorothy! Yes, she was moved by his manner of speech, the gentleness, the respect he gave her regarding her ministry that evening, and by his handsome looks!

Not knowing who the gentleman was, Dorothy went on to enquire (though it had to be said that it came out purely unintentionally), "Do you come here regularly?"

"No, not I; but my sister comes occasionally. She asked me to come tonight and tell her all about your message. She was not well enough to be here herself."

"Oh!" said Dorothy with some genuine concern. "I'm sorry to hear that."

Dorothy paused, wondering what else to say to the gentleman, for indeed she found words difficult under the circumstances, when he suddenly introduced himself as David Osborne.

"I do hope she will be better soon, David, and perhaps something you tell her about the meeting will bless her."

"Yes! I am sure so! Thank you! I will tell her what you have said."

Dorothy wished David good evening and thanked him for coming over to speak to her the way he had.

"It was my pleasure," he resounded spontaneously, with great fervour.

As Dorothy walked away, heading straight for home, she was quite oblivious of the fact that her recent acquaintance had remained motionless, seemingly transfixed to a particular spot on the carpet in the middle of the church aisle, staring at her figure until she was completely out of sight.

Dorothy soon arrived home, and opening the door to her flat, stepped up the few stairs and went straight into her lounge. A distant memory of a few months earlier engaged her thoughts as she began to make her tea. She was thinking of a certain Friday, having just returned from work, and the experiences of that particular evening.

"How amazing!" she thought aloud. "Who could believe that I would be speaking at a church meeting? I think Maria was right; this is awesome!"

At one point in the evening, whilst resting with a cup of tea, Dorothy ran through all the events of the meeting from beginning to end, rather like the rewinding of a video recording that had captured everything that had happened and was now playing it back upon the screen of her mind.

Upon reaching the conversation she had had with that gentleman called David, she paused and pondered it, thinking to herself, *Hm ... I liked David! I liked David very much!*

Chapter 8

John and Miriam Discuss Church Matters

John Peterson, the pastor, and Miriam, his wife, were still in the hall at the church. A few people had stayed behind talking and generally socialising. One convenient aspect, after such a meeting, was the opportunity it gave everyone to catch up with friends and all those with whom one might only tend to meet on a Sunday. However, this was not the sole reason why people stayed behind. There were always those who wished perhaps to talk to someone about the ministry having been challenged or illuminated whilst others stayed for whatever reason they may have wished to do so. Sometimes you might observe the pastor and or his wife quietly praying with someone over in a discrete part of the church.

Eventually, the stewards had finished tidying up the hall. The offering monies had been counted and band instruments with their associated electronic equipment and leads put away. Then finally, all the guests and groups of regular members had left the hall.

John and Miriam turned off the heaters and lighting and, being the last to leave, locked up the building. They too could now depart for home, it being about half an hour or so after Dorothy had done so.

The following evening, Miriam and John were sitting opposite one another in a large lounge close to a gas fire that was burning warm and cosily.

They had finished their supper that had consisted of a thick, brown, seeded toast and butter – a favourite of John's in the evenings – and they were now relaxing with a cup of English breakfast tea and reflecting upon recent events.

John was a warm, simple-natured man in his mid-fifties and had pastored the church for ten years. His doctrinal views were equally simple; he preached the Bible as it was written. He loved young people and had a passion for close up photography.

Miriam, however, loved her home and enjoyed cooking, especially cakes. Consequently, it naturally followed that she liked to entertain people in her house by cooking a meal for them.

"What did you think of Dorothy on Sunday evening, My Dear?" asked Miriam as John was just beginning to close his eyes in deep relaxation.

"Oh!" said John startled, "What did you say?"

Miriam repeated herself.

"I thought she was very good. In fact... very good indeed, I must say," replied John gradually increasing in emphasis as he spoke.

He rarely ventured into exuberant descriptive language or ever got excited about things, except perhaps when he was preaching, and then he would become quite a different personality. In fact, friends often referred to John's exuberance on such occasions as that of a fountain of water gushing out!

His reply to Miriam's question regarding Dorothy was verging upon being quite generous by his standards.

"Well, I thought she was absolutely marvellous, in fact exhilarating and wonderful," replied Miriam, determined to use even more expressive words than her husband. "To think that she has only been at our church for just a few months, and as far as I know never went to any other before that. What a change and transformation she has experienced; what tremendous ministry she has brought to us!"

"Well, the church needs such young people as Dorothy," replied John who was really in full and total agreement with his wife's opinion. "And not before time either! We had gradually become too familiar and predictable in our meetings as they stood but Dorothy…!"

John paused, not knowing her full name, and glancing towards his wife, beckoned to be enlightened.

"McGuire," said Miriam, "I spoke her name, *Dorothy McGuire,* loud and clear when introducing her that evening, My Dear!"

"Well, yes, of course," continued John. "Dorothy McGuire is a new inspiration to the church. Just look how many people attended last evening – and large numbers of young people too. More importantly, she spoke accurately and well, I thought. Very mature understanding for such a young one I would say."

"Thank you, Dear," replied Miriam, quite in agreement if not proud of her husband's analysis and opinion. "I couldn't agree more!"

John was just about to visit the bathroom when Miriam asked a further question. "There is just one more thing I really need to discuss with you, John; is now a good time?"

"Well… yes, Dear, of course; just give me a moment."

John soon returned. "Ok! Here I am," he said, attentive again to hear what his wife was about to say to him.

"Well, we really need to discuss upcoming visits," replied Miriam.

Both John and Miriam usually arranged for visits to certain people in the church each week and consulted one another as to who might be the most appropriate person to send. Most of the visits were to those who were sick, but sometimes there were other needs too. Of late, there was an increase of newcomers to the church and amongst them were some with particular needs. Miriam wished to discuss with her husband who would be appropriate to send in these cases.

"On Sunday evening," began Miriam, "there was a stranger in church, a gentleman. His sister apparently visited us once, but we have not seen her for a good while. Well, she is apparently now separated from her husband and lives with her young daughter not far from here. In fact, I do believe she lives in the vicinity of Dorothy's home, or somewhere out that way. What do you think about the idea of asking Dorothy if she would be interested in paying this lady a visit? They are both of similar age and I know from experience that Dorothy has a good empathy with ladies – especially those with particular problems or difficulties. She has experienced not a few herself, though perhaps not exactly in this particular realm."

John mused for a moment, rubbing the current days' growth of whiskers on his chin, thoughtfully regarded the proposition put to him. Finally, he responded and said, "I agree that such a person would have to be carefully chosen, Dear. It needs to be a lady and well…, yes, if Dorothy is of the same age as the person you are referring to, it just might be a good thing for her."

"Good for whom, for Dorothy or the lady?" Miriam added.

"Why, good for Dorothy of course! Who is the lady anyway?" asked John curiously.

"The gentleman, can you believe, forgot to mention her name, only that she had attended the church in the past. However, he gave us her address and phone number and assured me it would be quite alright for someone to visit her, as she rather likes the idea. Perhaps she gets lonely like so many do. He did sound very concerned for his sister.

"He stipulated that the person visiting her should phone first and arrange a convenient time for a visit, as I believe she takes her daughter to nursery in the morning and collects her in the afternoon."

John resorted to rubbing his chin again still in thought, for he did not have any strong view either way at this point regarding the matter, but was happy Miriam had consulted him nevertheless.

"I think your opinion on these matters is far weightier than mine, Dear. Thanks for telling me about the lady; I agree with your suggestion about Dorothy being an appropriate person to send, but please ask her if she would like to do this visitation and to keep us both informed about the lady."

How amicably this had been discussed and agreed! thought Miriam. Now it was just a matter of speaking to Dorothy about it.

"I will ask Dorothy," said Miriam happily, bringing the matter to a close.

The following day, during the late afternoon, John was again relaxing upon the sofa taking a break with a cup of his favourite tea which was, as usual, the English breakfast variety – irrespective of the time of day.

He was thinking over various church matters that needed to be resolved, but the item that concerned him most was regarding the recent discussion with his wife about visitations. John felt pressed to talk through his reservations with Miriam, and this he sought to do straight away.

"Are you there, Dear?" called John quite loudly.

"Only in the kitchen," replied Miriam.

"If you are not too busy, I would like to have a quick word with you; something has come to mind."

John's voice was considerably lower in volume and gentler in tone than previously, now that he was aware of his wife's whereabouts. A further response came from the kitchen, "Just one moment, John, and I will be with you. I am preparing the tea and coffee rota. I've almost finished."

The matter that concerned John was regarding Dorothy's involvement in the visitation program.

Now John and Miriam had a daughter called Rebecca, who on more than one occasion demonstrated views and opinions quite different to those of her parents. John loved Rebecca and had developed sensitivity towards young people as a direct result of being the father of one. Past experience had demonstrated that what seemed obvious or acceptable to him may not necessarily be considered in the same light by his daughter! Rebecca's thoughts and opinions as she grew up – her attitudes, likes, dislikes – were all so easily influenced and formulated by those of her contemporaries and were, on occasion, in stark contrast to those of her parents. John's concern was simply this, what would Dorothy, being a young person, really think about the idea of getting involved in a church visitation programme? Not really knowing Dorothy, John presupposed that she could well be of a similar mind to that of his daughter.

It was not long before Miriam's footsteps were heard coming into the lounge. Having entered she joined her husband upon the sofa; then, pouring herself a cup of tea, she asked, "Well, John, what is on your mind?" Almost in the same breath and still preoccupied in her thoughts by her recent task she continued, "I am so pleased to have finished that job. Do you know, John, there are not so many people as I had imagined that we can choose from."

John held his breath and waited patiently for a few seconds, acknowledging in his mind the importance of coffee and tea rotas, then took the next quiet moment to change the subject.

"Miriam," enquired John thoughtfully, "I was just thinking about our young people and how they like to do things together, you know… fun things like going out bowling and organising social events. Generally doing, I suppose, all the normal things people do at that age."

"Yes, Dear," replied Miriam, prompting John to get to the point with her body language.

"Well …" continued John hesitatingly, "Oh dear, how can I put this without saying the wrong thing? Do you think that asking a young person to visit a complete stranger is a good thing?"

"You mean Dorothy," said Miriam, anticipating that this must be the person referred to by her husband.

"Well, yes, I do mean Dorothy," replied John with apprehension. "What I really mean to say is this. Is it appropriate for Dorothy to engage herself in visiting people when she is quite young and new to the church? I suppose I am also thinking about Rebecca's possible reaction, Dear, if the same proposition would have been put to her. I fear maybe she would not have been particularly interested in this sort of thing, and I am a little concerned in case Dorothy's response about visiting someone might also be similar to hers. I mean, do you think, forgive me for saying so, that such a task for Dorothy might not be considered exhilarating enough for a vibrant young person like her? After all she is not that much older than our young people assuming she is in her early twenties, and I cannot for the life of me imagine them wanting to take up such a request! Would Dorothy wish to do so?"

At this point Miriam would not pass her opinion but became thoughtful too. Having listened very carefully to her husband, she partly wondered herself if this was a legitimate concern that he had expressed, and so she became quite flexible in her own mind about the whole matter.

"Yes, I know what you mean, John, and I think I agree with you. Dorothy is in fact 28 years of age by the way! I can assure you, however, that Dorothy is not the same person as our dear Rebecca. I happen to know that she is a very mature and caring person who thinks outside of herself, but she is new in the church, and it would not be fair to thrust this upon her so soon. Thank you for bringing this up, John. You have been very thoughtful about the matter. I must confess that I had not thought about it quite as deeply as you have."

John acknowledged his wife's remark graciously, and he became quite pleased with himself for raising his concerns with her.

"Times have changed considerably," added Miriam further, "and it tends to be much older people who take on board the ministry of visitation, especially as it could involve praying with people who might be ill for example. The fact that we did these things at their age is now irrelevant, and we need to think about what is appropriate for our young people today."

Miriam paused deep in thought for a moment, and then came up with a proposition to put to her husband.

"I tell you what, John," said Miriam impulsively and with considerable excitement. "Let us phone Dorothy now and ask her if she could come over and have dinner with us. What do you say?"

John, thinking this to be a rather sudden plan but a wonderful idea nevertheless, immediately answered in the affirmative and added his words of wisdom, "We will move more slowly with her in this matter."

Miriam disappeared into another room to make a phone call to the young lady in question, then immediately returned to her husband.

"Well, guess what?" smiled Miriam. "Dorothy is free tomorrow evening! She will come over straight after work. I just caught her, as she was just about to go out bowling with the young people."

"Bowling!" exclaimed John. "Well, there you are!"

John looked at Miriam with a sense of satisfaction, grinning with glee at this revelation that he may have accurately assessed the situation regarding the favoured youthful activities of the current generation after all! He found this information regarding Dorothy's association with the young people that evening particularly interesting, especially in the light of the discussion that had just taken place regarding visitation programmes and who to appoint.

"It seems that our Dorothy is no exception to the rest of the young people, after all, in her extra curricula activities!"

"Of course she is no exception, dear husband; how could you imagine for one moment she could be? But when you know Dorothy a little more in the same way that I do, you will then understand what I mean when I speak of her as having much maturity, for she has experienced much. She is one who can relate with empathy to women's problematic situations. In short, Dorothy is fun loving, yes, and this is needful in measure for one so young and in her condition. However, she is many other things too!"

Chapter 9

Tenpin Bowling

That very same day, two certain persons were each in their respective rooms in their respective homes preparing themselves to go out. Having showered and dressed, Maria Townsend, the recent acquaintance and friend of Dorothy, was adding final touches to her appearance as young ladies do, and was now almost ready for her lift.

The second person was the young man providing the lift, an Ian McPherson, the drummer in the church band. He was one year older than Maria and had just passed his driving test. Ian had also showered himself, gotten dressed and was adding the final touches to his appearance as young men would do, especially when picking up a girl.

Now, Maria was the more demonstrative of the two and more mature than Ian in spite of being a year younger in age. They had known each other since they were both very young children and were, it had to be said, quite good friends. Unofficially, Maria considered Ian as her boyfriend; and Ian, having always liked Maria, dare not act or say otherwise. This was their informal understanding of one another at this fresh and young time of their lives.

It was slowly getting dark when a bright red vehicle could be seen steadily driving towards its destination, albeit slightly later than anticipated.

A doorbell rang, and a man answered the door. Having gathered that it was Ian, he spoke gruffly.

"Hello. It's you, is it? Where do yeh think yer takin' my daughter this time?"

"We're going bowling, Mr Townsend," replied Ian nervously.

"You got wheels then, have yeh? It looks alright too. How much did that cost yeh then?"

"I'm not sure. My dad got it for me for my eighteenth birthday. I think it was somewhere round £500 to £600."

"Well, yer a lucky..." Various words followed that were unedifying to the ears of many, but fortunately for Ian, Maria came running down the stairs to meet her friend much to his relief.

"Sorry to keep you waiting, Ian. I was in the bathroom. Let's go. Bye, Dad!" And off they went like a shot.

Ian proudly held the car door open for Maria, and she sat in the front next to him. Having expressed her delight in seeing Ian's new car and being given a lift, Maria complimented his smart-casual dress and then in the same breath added, "Yes, Maria, you do look nice tonight too! Ian, you are supposed to say things like that to a girl!"

Ian, knowing Maria very well, took her reprimand gallantly and in a mature manner, which was quite out of place. Then, he turned slightly, smiled and handed her a rose that had been hidden under his seat, repeating her own words back to her!

"Yes, Maria, you look lovely tonight!"

"Ha! You're a sweetie, Ian. Thank you very much." From that particular moment, as they were driving to the bowling alley, the pair got on very well indeed!

On arrival at the steps of the bowling alley, Maria and Ian met Dorothy and two other young people from church. It was the first time that Dorothy had been out with other people for ages, and the last time she had been tenpin bowling must have been all of ten years ago during her teenage years!

Upon entering, Dorothy was very surprised and taken aback by what confronted her eyes. In the past, her experience of such a place was that of lots of bowling lanes, probably a café or a simple food and drink kiosk, and toilets – and that would have been the sum total! This time things were looking very different.

The light was subdued. A large amusement arcade was to the right and a table tennis area next to it. Coming into view over to the left was a complex area of pool tables, all of different sizes according to one's age. Beyond this pool area over in the distance, some sort of laser game was taking place. Adjacent to the pool tables was a carpeted area that went up two stairs to a bar positioned attractively in an arc. The appearance was not unlike a stage setting. Adjacent to the bar area, just a few feet away, was a café with tables and chairs neatly positioned and mostly occupied. This alone presented an appealing area of relaxation and fun, but the bowling lanes were yet to appear!

The party, having advanced thus far, came to an abrupt halt. Before them was the queue to obtain lane shoes, as ordinary footwear was forbidden. Once this task was accomplished and the party had moved forward, the bowling lanes finally came into view.

Streams of blue pulsating lights flickered up and down the edges of each lane like laser beams. Dorothy became excited and exclaimed to Maria, who by now had left her escort and was walking alongside Dorothy arm in arm, "Maria, this is quite amazing!"

Maria shrieked aloud ecstatically, "Wow! Fantastic!"

None of the party was particularly that experienced at tenpin bowling! The initial excitement slowly diminished and was replaced by frustration. What followed was the occasional lucky strike or two, and then shots that missed completely and ended up rolling down the gutter. Dorothy reminded everyone that it was a game and fun, for she had reacted with great humour when seeing balls taking to the side lanes; however, not everyone shared her light-heartedness!

After the bowling had concluded, there was pool; after the pool, there was coffee or coke; then there was table tennis!

When the evening was about three hours spent, Dorothy could be seen sitting and resting, feeling quite tired. The time was getting late, and everything closed down at midnight. It had to be said that stress in any shape or form would eventually take its toll on Dorothy's condition, and that included enjoying yourself and all the excitement that goes with it. Normally she would go to bed early, especially after a busy, day but not this particular evening. Many people were beginning to leave and so did the party in question. There was some sort of commotion going on ahead of them judging by the sound of things. People were shouting argumentatively.

"What's going on up there?" said Ian.

"Oh dear, it sounds like fighting! Too much to drink probably," replied Maria. As they moved closer to the commotion, Dorothy became quite alarmed and froze at what happened next!

Ian was knocked to the floor. He recognised a young boy who was clearly hurt, and in moving over to help found himself on the receiving end of the fight! Pandemonium erupted. Some people were screaming and pushing, as bodies seemed to be knocked in every direction. Everyone else just wanted to get outside and away from it all, but the exit corridor had narrowed thus causing a bottleneck squashing everyone together. Suddenly, Dorothy inadvertently took a wayward blow to her head and was down too. Maria shrieked and quickly came to the rescue, helping a dazed and bewildered Dorothy to her feet, whilst other members of the party helped Ian, pulling him away out of the trouble zone. His nose was bleeding profusely, and as he turned aside to look for his friends, Ian was attacked a second time.

Out of nowhere appeared the strong, constraining arms of several uniformed police officers, intervening and pulling both parties away. About eight young men – with Ian among them – were taken outside and pushed into a large van to be driven away.

Maria simply could not believe what was happening. It was like a horrid dream that surely could not be true. She gazed at the scene completely spellbound, watching Ian being ushered into the back of the van! Maria then ran towards the van shouting distraughtly with panic and utter disbelief, but it was too late ... Ian was gone!

The van disappeared out of view; then Maria remembered poor Dorothy! Turning aside, Maria temporarily forgot about Ian and ran over to Dorothy in panic, "How is she?"

Dorothy's friends were holding her; she was dazed and possibly suffering from a concussion. As Maria was running over to Dorothy, a gentleman suddenly came on the scene. Appearing from nowhere, he went over to where Dorothy was lying. Reaching into his pocket, he retrieved a mobile phone and made a call.

"She needs to go to hospital to be checked out. I have phoned for an ambulance."

Maria felt consoled by the strangers help. Someone needed to take control.

"How will you get home?" enquired the man, speaking to Maria.

"I can give her a lift," replied a friend from the party. "I know where Ian keeps the key. He puts it in a magnetic box under the chassis." This was agreed, though Maria insisted they follow the ambulance to the hospital in order to be with Dorothy.

Blue lights were flashing along the busy main road in the vicinity of the bowling alley, and in anticipation the stranger waved the ambulance over to where they were. The paramedics quickly checked Dorothy over before attempting to move her slumped body.

Reassuringly, one of them said she was basically fine but needed to be looked over. She had a mild concussion, but her pulse and blood pressure were fine. She looked as if she had received a heavy blow to the side of her head, maybe from a hard object, and would probably need an x- ray. That was their initial assessment at any rate.

The stranger gently touched Dorothy's hand as she was stretchered into the ambulance and seemed to mutter a few words over her before turning away to leave.

"What about Ian?" exclaimed a worried Maria to the man, stopping him in his tracks for he was walking away. Maria had suddenly redirected her concern now back to her boyfriend.

"I am going over to the police station now to see if I can be a witness. I saw everything. Is that the boy's name? Ian?"

"Yes… Ian; he is my boyfriend."

"Well, Maria, try not to worry too much. I will see to it and bring him home if I can."

"That is very kind of you. Who are you? A friend of Dorothy's?"

By now the gentleman was quickly walking away again, but he turned to Maria and replied, "Yes, a friend; you take care."

After saying these words, the gentleman was gone as quickly as he had come.

Chapter 10

Dorothy Confides in the Petersons

It was two weeks after the incident at the bowling alley. Dorothy had left the hospital to go home that very same evening, howbeit it was in the early hours of the morning, with a clean sheet. Being totally exhausted, she had taken two pain killers prescribed at the hospital, and then gone straight to bed.

Ian amazingly had appeared on the scene some two hours or so after the ambulance had taken Dorothy to the hospital. The stranger had dropped him off there having secured his release from the station. Ian had been advised to get checked out in 'Accident and Emergency' just to be on the safe side. Apparently the police had found no trace of drugs or alcohol in Ian's bloodstream, which was more than could be said of others, and the presence of the gentleman and his testimony had secured Ian's release without charge.

Having waited two to three hours to be seen by a doctor, Ian, when called in, took no longer than ten minutes. He had left the 'A&E' department and headed straight for Dorothy's ward. Upon finding Maria, Dorothy and his friend there, he had waited with them until they were released, then taken them all home.

The day now in question involved a belated dinner invitation for Dorothy at the Peterson's. It was quite a busy day for Miriam. Since a guest was coming to dine with them, she had decided to make a stew for the evening meal and bake an apple crumble with either custard or cream. These preparations she had done first thing in the morning, before the phone began ringing and duty called.

John was in his study preparing thoughts for coming ministries that week and the following Sunday. In the earlier years of his ministry, he would spend much time busying himself for these preparations by reading books, commentaries and other peoples' works, seeking to ensure that he had a good message to preach! Since then he had grown to realise that it was far better and easier simply to speak what he felt was appropriate and upon his heart. Consequently, John could be seen sitting in his study spending the time being quiet and prayerful.

When preaching, he always gave encouragement and direction in what he considered to be the biggest priority of all, namely to pursue relationship rather than religion. He emphasised that your purpose in life and destiny can only be found in God by knowing His love, learning His ways and His thoughts. John believed there was nothing more valuable than having this inner knowledge in your heart. He loved emphasising these convictions to young people in particular, as they always enquired about things in a simple practical manner, were not used to religious formalities, and were very receptive to that which added substance and reality to their life.

He noticed the time was steadily drawing close to six o' clock and that Dorothy would be arriving soon. John had received strict orders from his wife to ensure that the house was clean and tidy, and in particular, that his slippers, spectacles and newspapers were placed appropriately!

Meanwhile, Miriam had been doing her share of visiting that afternoon and intended to be home by 5.00 to 5.30pm. However, she was running late.

John was observing the tidiness of the lounge area, scrutinising it meticulously, when the telephone rang simultaneously with the chime of the doorbell. He dashed to the door to let Dorothy in, greeting her hurriedly and requesting she make herself comfortable in the lounge; then, in the very same breath, excused himself and ran to answer the telephone. It was Miriam on the phone, and after a few minutes of conversation, John placed the phone down and went over to where Dorothy was sitting in the lounge and explained to her just what his wife had requested he do.

"Miriam said to make you a drink and keep you company for a little while until she comes home. Apparently poor Mrs Ashley has had a fall, and Miriam is with her still. Well, how are you, Dorothy?" said John with a warm smile having regained his breath. "What a dreadful situation you were in at the bowling alley, Dear! How are you now?"

"Thank you, Mr Peterson, for your concern. I am quite well now. It was very traumatic at the time, but I thank God for helping me through it all."

John went on to fulfil his wife's directive, and after continuing with the normal formalities of welcoming a guest, he asked Dorothy if she would like a cup of tea.

"A tea would be lovely, thank you," replied Dorothy who had already seated herself upon a large settee facing a warm fire and was observing the large room with its elegant decor. There were candlesticks symmetrically positioned on either side of the mantle shelf. Above the mantle hung a large painting of an arched bridge over a pond full of lilies. Her reverie was interrupted by John's voice entering the room, informing her that tea was ready. He moved to sit adjacent to Dorothy.

Having noticed that Dorothy had been absorbed with the painting, John added, "That is Monet's *The Water Lily Pond* if you did not know, though only a replica unfortunately. I do love the beautiful pastel green colours; don't you?"

"Yes, I do. I do very much so," she replied with some depth of feeling, being quite absorbed by its beauty.

John had been waiting for an opportunity to thank Dorothy for speaking to the young people at church, but all opportunities to do so had evaded him, that is, until now.

"Well, Dorothy, I did appreciate your contribution to the meeting on that Sunday evening. Thank you. You did very well. I believe Miriam has received much positive feedback from more than one person. Well done!"

John spoke in a somewhat patronising manner at times, not adequately differentiating between a very young person and someone in their late twenties, but he always meant well and never inferred any sense of superiority. On the contrary, John was quite a humble and simple-natured man. He tended to speak as he felt and would be the first to admit that this sometimes did have repercussions. Dorothy, being a respectful and gracious person, showed no adverse effect from John's mannerisms towards her. In fact, she was very happy with his warm complimentary intentions and thought it rather nice to be addressed in a sort of fatherly manner.

"I thoroughly enjoyed speaking at church," she replied.

After a short interlude when all conversation had temporarily ceased, John changed their discourse into a fairly serious one. His voice altered to a very gentle whispering tone as he decided to address Dorothy in a more personal manner regarding her well-being and her past before becoming a Christian.

"I do believe you have had some difficult times previously, Dorothy. Please forgive me, I do hope this is alright for me to say this to you, but I do wish you to know how blessed Miriam and I are to have you with us. And it would be our honour and privilege to try and help you in any way you would wish us to do so. I can only say that whatever situation you may have been in before, you are an inspiration to all of us."

Dorothy was taken aback a little by John's openness in the former part of his remark and was only pleased he had not continued to ask anything more of her. Even so, she perceived that his intention was of genuine concern and was pleased by the kindness displayed in the latter part of his remark, so much so that she became in need of the use of her tissue which was kept tucked away as usual.

At this, John was also taken by surprise at Dorothy's reaction and apologised if he had spoken insensitively.

"No, not at all, Pastor. I am perfectly fine, thank you," she replied with an air of formality. "You are right. I have had some difficulties in the past, and now I am gradually… well of late, getting over them little by little. You have a right to know something about me perhaps, but I would rather not pursue the subject any more just now if that is alright with you."

Dorothy believed it was the correct thing to be politely assertive with John at this time, whether he was her host or not. She was alone with a man she hardly knew and had not spoken to anyone except Miriam about her private life.

John blushed slightly with embarrassment, realising the matter was far too sensitive, and felt guilty for bringing it up in the first place!

"Please accept my apologies, Dorothy, for being an over-enquiring, insensitive nincompoop! Never feel any sense of obligation on my part to say anything personal to me, Dear," stressed John. "I only know a little of what Miriam told me, namely that you have experienced some difficulties, though what they are I do not know, neither do I wish to know anything without your permission."

Little did John realise that Dorothy would never feel any sense of obligation to say anything to him if it was not in her mind to do so, but she felt it best to refrain from mentioning that particular thought of hers.

At this point, the conversation came to an end as Miriam came in through the door.

"So sorry for being late," she uttered, slightly out of breath. Miriam moved over to Dorothy, who was standing to meet her, and greeted her with a warm hug.

"How are you, Dorothy? I'm so pleased you could come over this evening, and oh! I was so sorry to hear about what had happened to you, Dear! Are things better now for you?" Dorothy went for a second hug with Miriam and gently said words to the effect that she was much better.

Glancing around at the room, Miriam quickly inspected it to see how clean and tidy everything was, then thanked John for tidying it up.

"Now, would you be able to help me in the kitchen, Dorothy?"

"Yes, of course," she replied with enthusiasm, and they both left the room immediately, leaving John by himself.

There is clearly an atmosphere of proactivity and an injection of life in the house now that Miriam has arrived home, thought John, *not the least in the direction of the kitchen. Certainly the food smells good!* A meaty aroma was permeating through into the lounge.

John sat back in his chair rather pleased with himself for having cleaned the house to Miriam's satisfaction! He had a wonderful wife, a wonderful guest, and the anticipation of a wonderful dinner about to be served! How good was his feeling at that precise moment – a fair definition of satisfaction with contentment! However, in order to check himself so as not to take all of this comfort and provision for granted, he determined within himself to ensure that he did the washing up afterwards though this was not really necessary as Miriam would inevitably call upon his help in this direction anyway!

John also determined in his mind to only speak at the table that which was edifying and acceptable. He considered this a matter he must get right, for the slight sting of Dorothy's response to him earlier had not yet passed away.

The time finally arrived; the stew was ready for the threesome, and the three were ready for the stew.

Such occasions as these were most acceptable to Dorothy. She relished the family atmosphere of sitting around the table together to have a meal, and she could not remember the last time when she had done anything similar in the past. Mealtimes spent with other people were usually held in a restaurant or café and never in the simple comfort of a home, so this was very special to her; there was no place like home after all!

The stew had disappeared in total after second servings were made all-round, as did the apple crumble that followed. *Surprisingly,* thought Miriam, *Dorothy asked for custard upon it and not cream!*

After the meal was finished, Miriam insisted John and Dorothy venture into the lounge saying she would bring in the coffee. John's intention regarding the washing up did not materialise at this point, as – by strict orders from Miriam – the dishes were to be left until later, the entertainment of their guest taking supremacy over this common chore.

Passing through to the lounge, Dorothy perched herself upon the sofa just as before, facing the Monet painting, whilst John seated himself upon an armchair. It was a very relaxing ambience, and John, having stretched out lazily, addressed Dorothy in a casual, light-hearted but nevertheless careful manner asking her about more recent times.

"Your work, Dorothy… what exactly do you do?"

"Well, Pastor…" John cut her short,

"Oh, do call me John if you will."

"Well, John, I work in market research," continued Dorothy, "at Johnson's Corporation."

"Wow!" said John. "That sounds good, but er… what exactly does that involve if I may ask?"

Dorothy smiled at this point because of John's apparent ignorance and because he was openly unashamed of it. She proceeded in giving him a simple definition. Dorothy was in her element talking quite comfortably with John, and in doing so she got to know him better. She observed and learned of a personality rare and pleasant.   John was indeed a very simple-minded man with a quality that was real and genuine. Rarely had she known a person to be so. He presented an open door of trust and honesty, welcoming anyone to speak freely and even confide in him if they had a mind to do so. The outcome was a Dorothy who now felt much safer and at ease with John, and her earlier reservation toward him was mellowing.

Miriam had by now entered the lounge with drinks for everyone. Realising that their conversation had clearly progressed to informality if not joviality, Miriam also took on a light-hearted, joking manner when she added, "It seems you two are now quite amicably acquainted with one another; may I now join you both if that is not too intrusive?" Her remark triggered rapturous laughter all round.

This warm atmosphere with gentle humour was a unique occurrence for Dorothy who, perhaps for the first time in many years, felt at ease in a safe environment with two people whom she both now respected and trusted, and who were becoming very dear to her. She felt no hesitation or embarrassment to talk or share with them both, and in response to a request from Miriam to talk about herself a little, she began with what was to be a long discourse of her life up until the present.

Dorothy started at the beginning.

"I was brought up as an only child in Dorset, right in the heart of its rural countryside. I very rarely saw much of my father for months at a time since, he was in the Merchant Navy and based in Plymouth. I do remember hearing my parents arguing together quite a lot from my bedroom as a small child. Sometimes my mother would cry; I used to run to her, and we would embrace one another. I loved mother very much, and she always wanted the very best for me. She sent me to private schools and financed my university education for which I feel very privileged and grateful. As you know, I now work for a large company in market research, though I was originally qualified in information technology and worked in programming for three years in Bath."

"Which university did you go to, Dorothy?" enquired John.

"Oh, I was able to get in at Oxford," she replied.

"Very nice," added Miriam emphasising the word *very* and thus highlighting, without actually saying so in words, her appreciation that this was a great achievement on Dorothy's part. "How was your relationship with your father?" continued Miriam.

At this point in her discourse, Dorothy paused and looked across making eye contact with Miriam as if to ask, *Should I really talk about this?*

Miriam, reading Dorothy's thoughts very clearly, added quickly, "Only say what you feel comfortable with, Dorothy."

Miriam was already aware of quite a lot of what was a very sensitive area in Dorothy's life, Dorothy having confided in her on a certain Sunday morning after the service. Her husband, however, did not know any specifics at all about the matter, so Miriam had purposely posed this question in order for Dorothy to have an opportunity to talk about her father, in as little or as much detail as she desired, and thus enlighten her husband. Miriam had considered that whatever Dorothy could feel comfortable saying openly regarding her father would only be of benefit to her.

Dorothy declared nervously that her relationship with her father had not been at all good. She went on to say how her father, when at home on leave, would usually come in drunk in the evening, and on such occasions would go into her bedroom under the pretence of kissing her goodnight.

Dorothy again paused nervously and gazed at the floor as if ashamed. Her countenance changed and revealed a subdued and serious expression; then, gradually she struggled emotionally with what she was about to utter. In a determined fashion, typical of her resilient character, she painfully recounted how her father would touch her! This had carried on for several years, whenever he would come home on leave.

Dorothy mentioned how she would keep asking her mother when her father was next coming home, and how relieved she became whenever her mother's answer was, 'Not for a good while, Darling.' But she had dreaded the times when told that his next visit was imminent! Dorothy's life had become a living nightmare during these years, and when the opportunity to go to boarding school had come, she had relished it – much to the surprise of her mother who knew nothing of her daughter's dreadful plight.

By now John's countenance had grown much paler, having listened intently to Dorothy's last words.

Miriam continued, "What about your parents now, My Dear?"

She genuinely enquired this time, not knowing herself of their whereabouts, whereas most of what Dorothy had said thus far was already known to her.

"Well, both of my parents have passed away now," replied Dorothy who, having bravely revealed the most difficult part, now appeared somewhat relieved at this point in her discourse to be able to direct attention to different subject matter. Howbeit, what was to follow was not exactly that much of an improvement to the revelations just disclosed regarding her father – revelations that had visibly alarmed and shaken John, who was still held spellbound by them as if in some shock!

Dorothy continued to answer Miriam's original question.

"My mother passed away a long time ago. After having a major operation, she contracted pneumonia, which took her. My father died rather tragically only about four to five months ago, and without my knowledge."

"Good gracious!" exclaimed John bursting with surprise. "That must have been round about the time we first met you, was it?"

"Yes, it was a week or two before I first came to the church that Sunday morning when I accidently discovered the news. Well, anyway, my address had changed three times; he had no idea of my whereabouts, and I confess that at that time I had no inclination or desire to contact him, or anyone else for that matter."

Dorothy couldn't help but weep with some degree of remorse at this point, but then continued to enlarge upon the tragic circumstances regarding her father's death in a brave and determined manner.

She had accidently read of her father's death in a newspaper!

"The article was at national news level," said Dorothy, "and I recognised the name of his ship which was *The Enterprise*. I was drawn to the headlines to read that several officers and crew members were killed when the ship ran aground on some rocks and listed to one side. He was amongst those who had been seriously injured, and the report said he died in hospital a few days later. I enquired in Plymouth at the Blue Funnel Company, because that was where he was stationed, and they informed me that the funeral was in a church near the docks. I went to attend the service, but I got lost in Plymouth, and by the time I arrived at the church it was all over and everyone had gone. So that was that, and here I am now!"

Dorothy had attempted to finish on a light-hearted note, but it had little effect in changing the subdued and sombre atmosphere created by the discourse of her dismal past and the circumstances surrounding the demise of both of her parents.

John gazed at Dorothy with new enlightenment and felt utterly gutted that she should have gone through such hurt, which was by his account beyond measure.

"Thank God you have come to us, Dorothy! Or perhaps it is closer to the truth to say you have been sent to us!" said John in his simple, spontaneous manner, attempting to find some positive words to say.

He stood to his feet quite overcome by his emotions, which put an end to his previous decorum and propriety. John's remark – with his kindly intentioned burst of thanks – had pierced the still and silent room with its lingering and sad atmosphere; it had recharged the air a little with energy and life once again.

Dorothy responded with equal emotion, and springing to her feet moved over in the direction of John to hug him warmly, or nearer to the truth to be hugged by him.

Sympathy, consolation and thoughts enriched with loving sentiments were held in high regard by Dorothy, and the words just spoken by John quite spontaneously regarding her circumstances had touched her heart.

A certain favourite scripture came to Dorothy's mind.

"A word fitly spoken is like apples of gold in settings of silver."

John had fulfilled that without realising it!

And so the evening culminated on this positive note with Miriam also embracing Dorothy, before she left on her journey home.

Both John and Miriam needed time and rest to contemplate all of the happenings that Dorothy had experienced. They hardly spoke to one another in the latter part of that evening; and John, after kissing his wife on her cheek, gently spoke to her saying, "I think that I will get ready for bed now."

As he moved towards the stairs he turned to utter some closing words. "We have heard quite a lot tonight. It will take some assimilating, I'm sure. God bless, Dear."

Within minutes Miriam traced her husband's steps and followed him to bed.

Chapter 11

Another Meeting in Town

The following morning, when John and Miriam were having breakfast together, Miriam reminded her husband that the original purpose for requesting Dorothy dine with them the previous evening had been completely forgotten, there being a more important and unknown agenda that had taken place instead. They had initially been intending to ask Dorothy about her possible interest in church visitations, but in retrospect the issue seemed to fade into insignificance in the light of what had actually taken place, and the unique opportunity that had arisen to listen to Dorothy open up her heart and give them much more understanding about her.

In order to address the outstanding need of visiting a certain lady with a little girl, Miriam decided upon a different strategy; it could be solved by doing the visitation herself in the first instance rather than asking Dorothy at this stage. She relayed this change of plan to her husband, who was in full agreement with her.

Having retrieved the phone number of the lady in question from her handbag, Miriam went over to the phone and arranged for a visit that very afternoon.

Meanwhile, John had ventured over to his study with the intention of meditating upon words and Scriptures from their morning reading. However, the words spoken by Dorothy in the Sunday evening service a few weeks earlier became uppermost in his mind and took precedence. They seemed to take on a new dimension of significance in light of her revelations, which had made a deep impression upon him.

For a young lady, who had experienced such misfortune, to talk about having a positive outlook and breaking down negative strongholds in one's life was quite remarkable, and her address to the church that evening carried much more weight now in the light of what he knew about her past than it had when he had first heard her speak – when he had simply thought she had acquired mature understanding for one so young and new in the faith. It seemed that her adverse experiences did not affect her preaching. She had a grasp and enlightenment of scriptures and spoke with boldness, authority, relating her words to practical situations that were able to meet people's needs. Indeed, it was as if her background had enhanced her ministry with authentic realism! It was one thing to preach upon a subject well, but quite another to have lived it and experienced it; Dorothy's preaching was so anointed and powerful!

John was fully aware that such ministry could not be achieved through human understanding or intellectual ability but only through the enabling, illuminating power of the Holy Spirit; and he, through his own personal experience acquired over many years, had come to realise that knowledge and revelation can only be imparted to the believer directly through a personal relationship with God and by dwelling in His presence. There was no substitute for this.

Over the years, it had become very clear in John's mind that a desire and hunger for God's love and to know Him through His Word and by His Spirit was about all one should aspire to. This yielding and submission was the only way to bring down the reality of His presence. It was without respect of persons, age, sex, earthly qualifications, social standing, or ministerial experience.

John was musing quite deeply within his own soul, still contemplating the recent challenge and enlightenment he had received regarding everything surrounding the person of Dorothy and her excellent ministry of the Word in spite of the incredible account of her background. 'One thing is for sure,' said John speaking aloud to himself and bringing his private meditations to a close. 'That girl, Dorothy, has much to give to young people – and adults too!'

Several days later, towards the end of that week, Miriam was to be found wandering through the high street in town, which was not too far away, only about ten minutes journey by car on a good day. It was a market town with friendly, pedestrianised areas full of a variety of shops, coffee bars, tea rooms and patisseries.

A small cobbled square stood set apart and secluded from the rest of town. It was surrounded by trees and had a fountain in the centre. It was the perfect spot for a quiet rest and relief from busy shopping, and Miriam headed in that direction sitting down upon a seat facing the fountain.

The sky was a nice blue with some patchy white clouds that were moved swiftly by a moderate wind. Miriam was staring at the large trees that were positioned at equal intervals around the perimeter. Several tree sparrows made their presence heard, fluttering in and out of the branches of a bushy tree, twittering away and creating a jungle-like sound as they congregated together making good use of this isolated haven. The wind carried a faint spray of mist as it blew against the rising water from the fountain, carrying it in the direction where Miriam was sitting. Miriam, not being too alarmed, simply shuffled to one side. Wood pigeons were busy warbling, nodding their heads and trotting along the ground feasting upon bread thrown out for them by others, who also sat in the square enjoying their lunchtime sandwiches.

What a beautiful day! thought Miriam, inhaling a deep breath of air whilst holding her head slightly back gazing at the sky. She found the scene before her very much to her liking.

She must have been sitting there a good ten minutes when the figure of a tall, elegant young lady entered the very same square and approached the very same bench upon which Miriam sat. When the lady sat next to her, Miriam turned and smiled, "Hello, Dorothy; I'm so pleased you could make it."

"Hello to you, too," retorted Dorothy very happily.

They conversed together for a while when Miriam changed the course and direction of their conversation more towards the reason and purpose for her meeting with Dorothy.

"Well now, how about going to that favourite coffee bar of ours for a latte? There is something I would like to tell you, but I am feeling like a coffee right now. What do you say?" If her beaming face was any indication, Dorothy was quite happy to go along with that arrangement!

They left the square and wandered in a direction leading them to at least three different choices of venue. Miriam asked Dorothy, "Do you remember the café we went to after we had been shopping and you bought yourself that nice purple top off the mannequin in the window?"

"Why, yes! I remember that well," replied Dorothy smiling. "It seems such a long time ago, and we had not long met one another then. Much water has gone under the bridge since that time."

Dorothy momentarily drifted back in her thoughts to the time in question when she had struggled into church and met Miriam who had helped her in so many ways. How, having met up together one day, Miriam had taken her out shopping, and they had stopped for a coffee.

Now the twosome once again entered the very same coffee bar – *Max's*. Dorothy's memory was revived. "Why, there is the round table near the window. I remember asking you if we could sit there!" exclaimed Dorothy.

"Yes!" replied Miriam. "And do you remember how you insisted on paying for that lady's drink – the one who was a complete stranger – and how you invited her to sit at our table? You both talked and talked for ages."

"I do indeed!" she replied, the very thought of this pleasant recollection still vivid in her mind.

Now, as they were sitting at the very same round table again drinking their coffee together, Miriam opened a particular topic of conversation. "You will never believe what I am going to tell you, Dorothy." She paused to sip her coffee and taste her fresh croissant as if deliberately wanting to delay the rest of the conversation for a short moment to keep her friend in suspense.

Dorothy was most inquisitive and eager to hear the substance of what Miriam was about to declare. "Please, tell me. What it is?" she replied with a growing sense of urgency.

Miriam placed her croissant down on the plate and continued at last. "Mm, how nice and fresh they are. Well, Dorothy, I went to see a lady today, and guess what? It was that very same person you were talking to."

"What! Do you mean the lady we met here?"

"Yes, that very same lady, Dorothy; I met her today!" Miriam munched again at her croissant. Because it was so fresh, there was the added inconvenience of the crumbs which fell all over her at each and every crunch.

"Well, how amazing!" exclaimed Dorothy. "And how is she?"

"Well, not without some difficulties," replied Miriam.

"How did this come about?" queried Dorothy. "Where did you see her?"

"I visited her at her home and recognised her as the same person we both had met that time in this very same café. She had apparently come to our church one evening a long time ago and enjoyed it very much, though we have no record of her having ever attended again. Well, last Sunday evening after your preaching, a gentleman who I have never seen before, came to speak to me about his sister who was not well and who would love to receive a visit from someone in our church."

Upon hearing this, Dorothy recollected how she had also been approached by a gentleman that evening. "I wonder if this was the same gentleman I met?" declared Dorothy thinking out aloud. "It sounds very much like it could have been, and if so, then he would have been her brother!"

"Well", continued Miriam, "as I said, the lady is not without difficulties. She is not at all well. There is a separation involved, and though she has the house as part of the arrangement of things, she also has care of a daughter. The whole episode has made her quite ill mentally. I think she should get some advice and support. I need to get someone to visit her occasionally just to be with her. She has shown an interest in this, but I need to get the right person to do it."

Whilst everything Miriam had expounded to Dorothy was absolutely true in every detail, she could not help but take advantage of the situation with the latter in her presence to stipulate the need for an appropriate person to visit this lady. She had left it open to see if Dorothy would react or not react accordingly regarding the matter. In short, Miriam had invited Dorothy to meet her that day to possibly lean upon her good nature for this very task, and she succeeded!

"Oh, Miriam!" exclaimed Dorothy, "If you are looking for someone to visit this lady, then I would love to do so myself – if that is acceptable to you, that is. I got on very well with her when we spoke together that time here in this café, and indeed at this very same table. I would really like to meet her again!"

Miriam, observing the sincerity of Dorothy's heart and her willingness to help without any obligation or sense of duty was taken somewhat by surprise. She now felt a little ashamed of herself. Whilst Miriam had hoped in her heart Dorothy might have shown some interest in the matter, there was something about her innocent and joyous response that brought about a sense of guilt within her, and she began to question her own motive about the whole arrangement. It had not been necessary to have sought to persuade or coerce Dorothy to visit the lady in question; she was only too pleased to do so, but the very thought of attempting this strategy brought about this sense of remorse in Miriam. Being who she was, Miriam could not but respond to Dorothy with some measure of humility and honesty.

"Dorothy", replied Miriam with a hint of contrition, "I have to say to you that John and I were wondering whether you would have been interested in visiting this lady, but we delayed asking you so that we could think about it. I must confess to you, dear Dorothy, that this was the sole reason I asked you to meet with me today; and I do apologise if I have pressured you to feel obligated to take on board this task, taking advantage of your good nature.

"I should have asked you perhaps in a more direct manner instead of beating about the bush. Please do not take on this commitment if you do not wish to do so. I am perfectly happy to deal with it myself. Please feel free to do this task, or equally, not to do it – as you wish."

Miriam felt somewhat better having presented this frank exposition to Dorothy, and the latter consoled the former that she need not worry or be concerned in any way. In fact, Dorothy asserted that were she not happy about the situation, she would have said so, and she couldn't help but wonder just why Miriam was going on for so long seemingly troubled about it!

It was finalised! The matter was settled! The two ladies had both had their say, and both were very happy with the outcome, though perhaps Miriam had learned something that she hadn't bargained for from the experience!

It was imperative, however, that Dorothy request some rather important and necessary information if the agreed undertaking was to be executed.

"Miriam, I will need to know the lady's address and phone number."

"Of course! I think that will be useful information, don't you?" replied Miriam with a chuckle, and then she quickly scribbled it down on some paper and pushed it along the table towards Dorothy.

"Oh, and by the way, what is the lady's name?"

"Mary," replied Miriam. "That is all I know."

Chapter 12

Alfred Townsend

Maria Townsend sat in her bedroom contemplating what to do with her life when suddenly her phone rang.

"Hi there, Maria; this is Dorothy."

"Hello, Dot, great to hear yer. How yer doin'?"

Maria had resorted to using the abbreviation of Dorothy's name, thinking it sounded better; and as no objection ever came back, it stuck.

"I'm good, thank you," said Dorothy. "I was thinking of coming round to see you, but thought I'd phone you first to see if it was convenient."

"No problem," replied Maria, "but just to warn you… my dad is home, and he's still givin' me grief for coming home so late you know, the night we went bowling; totally insane he is! Oh! I am so stressed at the moment, Dot; life totally sucks! I don't know what to do with my life, and there's my college course, right? That's going down the chute goodtime; then my dad? That's a joke! Somebody, help me please!"

Maria's alarm bells were not all they seemed; it was her way of getting off her chest those problems common these days to teenage mankind. Her vivid expressions regarding the causes of her *stress* were somewhere in between gross exaggeration and genuine need! There were solutions; she just needed help finding them.

"Oh my goodness!" said Dorothy with both shock and surprise. "Well, if it is opportune, I could perhaps speak to your dad. Then maybe we could both go out together for a coffee; what do you think?"

Maria audibly laughed over the phone. "Please do as you feel, Dorothy! It's worth a try, but beware... I have warned you! Yes, coffee sounds a fantastic idea; let's do that whatever happens!"

Now it was the case that Dorothy had already felt the need to give Maria's father a word of explanation about the night his daughter had arrived home exceedingly late. After all, Maria had been late on that particular evening because of her. Now, after hearing what Maria had said about receiving a lot of grief from her father, she realised that it was most needful to do so.

Upon hearing this comment and all of Maria's other troubles, Dorothy felt it all the more expedient to go and see her.

"See you soon Maria."

Fortunately, Mr Townsend had not been drinking that day, having been on his weekly visit to the hospital. He was his usual self – grumpy, edgy and of course, as gruff as can be.

He had little refinement, whether in good manners, conversation or anything else that might come to mind pertaining to a gentleman. No, Alfred Townsend was all brawn and no finesse.

Alfred had worked on his father's farm for 37 years. Starting at fifteen, he'd been forced to retire early through a tractor accident; it would not be expedient to amplify in detail just how this came about, suffice it to say he was left incapacitated in his left leg and could not work on the farm anymore.

This misfortune had brought about a drastic change to the outdoor lifestyle he had known. To this very day, some six to seven years later, he had not yet come to grips with the imposition it placed upon him. It had been a very sore point with Alfred in other ways, as well as physical ones! He had an argument with life itself for doing this to him, as he thought.

His wife had left the home to live with her sister, it being too much to bear. Alfred had not gotten better but worse, and it had gone on far too long for her liking.

Ironically, Maria had chosen to live with her father. To her, his *bark* was far worse than his *bite,* and it didn't bother her too much – though his well-being did. This parental affection of Maria's towards her dad was quite strong, probably because she inwardly knew her father cared about her, and she felt sorry for him. All the grief from him, as she would put it, and verbal moaning she received would be construed as his way of showing this care, in spite of the fact that he tried to be quite possessive with her.

Basically, Alfred only had Maria to be there for him, as selfish as this was. However, as a consequence, Maria did not take enough responsibility for her own self as much as she ought; this was the emotional pressure she found herself under. Some said it was like emotional blackmail or even abuse. After all, it was not Maria's fault that her father had a problem with drinking; neither was she to blame for her own mother's departure from the house. She was unfairly left to pick up the pieces. Where were the adults? Maria was left in the home she was born in, taking on board the responsibility of looking after her father. As a consequence, she was depriving herself of normal social activities, not the least her Further Education course at college, where she was seriously behind. The situation, left as it was in its current state, was a ticking time bomb.

Maria had decided to forewarn her dad regarding his behaviour and manners before her visitor arrived in order to minimise all embarrassment if that were at all possible. Consequently, she said to him in a firm, authoritative tone, "Dad, will you please watch how you speak and behave when Dorothy gets here?"

"Of course a will, Lass; what you expectin' of me?"

"Dad!" Maria heard her father's words but they did not register as being serious enough for her liking. "Dorothy is different to the rest of my friends. She is ... well, she is a lady, a mature person, you know! Promise me. Please, Dad? You will mind how you speak to her?"

"Alright, al promises to be careful what a say. Is that good enough for yeh?"

"Thank you." And at that Maria finished.

———

It was not long after Maria's reprimand to her father that the doorbell rang. It sure enough was Dorothy who had just arrived. Heartbeats raced momentarily, until Maria's friend had entered the room where Alfred was seated and introduced herself, "Hello Mr Townsend, I am very pleased to meet you."

"This, Dad, is my friend, Dorothy," chirped in Maria, conscious that so far all was going well and sensing a different atmosphere in the room with Dorothy's presence in it. Having seated herself upon a nearby chair, Dorothy came straight to point.

"I would like to say how grateful I was when your daughter kindly stayed with me in hospital one night a few weeks ago. I do hope you didn't mind her arriving home very late on that evening - or should I say, in the early hours of the morning. I can assure you that it was entirely on account of me."

Alfred was taken aback in surprise at what met his eyes and ears from the moment Dorothy had entered the room, seated herself and started speaking to him.

First of all, no one, he thought *is ever very pleased to see me!* Then he saw and observed intently that Dorothy was indeed a nice, genteel, ladylike sort of person, quite different to anyone else he knew! She was elegant, beautiful and all smiles, airs and graces. *Who is she?* Alfred thought to himself. *How did she come on the scene?*

It did not seem possible for this lady's path of life to cross his, and yet here she was!

Alfred, after Dorothy had confirmed the reason why Maria had arrived home late that night – though he had been told exactly the same thing by his daughter already – casually apologised to Maria, and then went on following the path of his own curiosity regarding Dorothy.

"So where yer from then, Dear? A mean how did yer meets up wi mi daughter?"

"Why, I live about ten minutes' drive away going out of town," replied Dorothy. "Regarding Maria, I had the delightful pleasure of meeting her in church one morning when I first attended several months ago."

"Ah! Church! That place brings all kinds together, don't it? I see! That explains it!"

Alfred, upon hearing this last statement from Dorothy, began from that time onwards to respect his own daughter's choice in going to church, for he felt that he could no longer gainsay it after hearing that this Dorothy also went to her church!

Thus far, he could not fault Maria's friend, who had come into his house to testify of his own daughter's integrity and to clarify to him the reason for her arriving home late! Alfred felt ashamed of himself that this situation should have had to come about. Why could he not have accepted his own daughter's words and reasons himself when she first told him? Instead, he had chosen the path of disrespect towards her by not receiving her words in the first place. He knew only too well just what grief he had given Maria, and now, as he sat in the presence of the two of them, he felt guilt and shame rising from within him. Attempting to shrug this off, Albert continued, "So, you goes to church as well do yeh?"

"Yes, I do, Mr Townsend. I did not always go, but I do now. I love going."

"Well, stone the crows! Seems to me women likes church, hey?"

"Well, what about you, Mr Townsend? Do you ever go to church?" Dorothy replied not at all perturbed by Alfred's comments.

"Me! What about me, do yeh say? I ain't been ta church some seven years nar. No, not me!" Alfred spoke firmly, decisively and very strongly.

"Why is that? Is it simply that you do not care to go?" asked Dorothy in an inquisitive manner, provoking Mr Townsend to explain his reasons.

"Do yer really wants to know why? 'Cos if yeh do, I'll tell thee! Because of mi leg yer see; because of what's a bin done to me!"

Alfred was now pointing in the direction of his injured leg with a facial expression that could only be described as exhibiting strong bitterness, seemingly because of his having to endure the injury in the first place, but also because he had grown quite resentful about it and the imposition it had placed upon him.

"That must have been awful for you, Mr Townsend! I am so sorry," replied Dorothy. "Does that mean you are unable to get out at all?"

Now, Dorothy had not discerned or understood Albert properly through her innocence and naivety, for he had ulterior motives other than his injured leg for not going to church – and these suddenly became clear and plain to all.

"Yeh don't get it, do yeh?" exclaimed Albert with a forceful tone of voice still pointing to his injured leg. "This can't be done to mi from any God o' luv, can it nar?"

Dorothy was taken aback and a little shaken by the sudden turn of events. It would seem she had inadvertently let loose a storm from within him by her innocent questioning. Even so, Dorothy knew all too well about suffering and pain and was not deterred in any way whatsoever by his obnoxious attitude and his blaming of God for his ailments. It was the same story heard so many times.

Now, Dorothy had rather strong opinions regarding this particular matter and was quite bold to speak on it.

"As I said, Mr Townsend, I am very sorry about what happened to you. It must be terrible to lose the use of your leg, but..." Dorothy paused before continuing with what she was determined to say. "...but many people have suffered in this world, including myself. We do have to learn how to move on in some way. I personally turned to the Lord in the thick of my problems, and He has helped and blessed me more than words could tell. Further, where was God, you might say, when Jesus was nailed to a cross?

"Was Jesus not in pain?! Yes! Of course He was, but there was a purpose, Mr Townsend; there was a Divine purpose as to why this was allowed. We do not always understand the *why* of every problem situation, certainly not at the time anyway. Mr Townsend, God never promised you and me that there would be no suffering in life, but He did promise, however, to be with us through them."

And so it was that Alfred received far more than he had bargained for from this genteel sort of ladylike person, and equally, Dorothy received more than she had anticipated from him too.

The hurt and resentment he had carried embedded deep within him over the seven years since his accident had festered like an untreated wound, so that this non-physical injury of bitterness and self-pity had grown with time, whilst the physical side of things had healed up years ago. Alfred's trauma had never been mollified with the balm of someone's love or words of encouragement and comfort.

Would Dorothy's words help him, or would they harden his heart even further?

Only time would tell.

Chapter 13

Dorothy's Advice to Maria

Dorothy was quite excited about going out with Maria, and, needless to say, Maria was ecstatic to be in Dorothy's company.

Having left Alfred to be by himself to ponder all the events of the last thirty or forty minutes, they both got into Dorothy's car and headed off into town.

Uppermost in Maria's mind was, more than likely, the same subject and contemplation as that of her father regarding all that had just been said. She had been shocked to hear her dad come out with so much, and was likewise just a little astonished with Dot's forthrightness in saying what she had said too.

"That was, like, awesome!" said Maria, commenting on what had just happened.

"Oh, was it? I am not too sure now in retrospect," replied Dorothy. "I felt I just may have sounded too hard or insensitive."

"I like, nearly died of embarrassment to hear dad goin' on, if you know what I mean! He's never said things like that before, you know. Well, like, not as heavy as that."

Dorothy smiled as she listened to Maria talk. Maria reminded her of herself as a teenager, speaking the way she did - accent and all.

"What is it then? What have I said?" chirped Maria, aware that something seemed to have just tickled her friend – and that something, she felt, was about her.

"Oh, it's like, just fine; really cool in fact or maybe even totally cool," said Dorothy sarcastically trying her utmost to imitate Maria's use of words and accent, but not doing a very good job of it as far as the accent was concerned!

"Dot, you sound so different talking like that! Just stick to *you* and *you* only, otherwise people will think you are a prize jerk. It don't like, sound right when you say that lingo, you know! You ain't in the club, are you? He... He!"

"Um..., I think I agree, Maria. Definitely! And thanks by the way for saying I sounded like a prize jerk!

"Actually, Maria, listening to you speak just now did remind me of something from years ago in school; that's why I was smiling, not because I was laughing at the way you spoke. There was this bouncy, cheeky sort of girl who was new in our class. I think she came from London, and her name was Sonia. Well, we all thought she spoke so differently – though she probably thought exactly the same about us I guess – you know, *talkin' like thart*, with a West Country accent and all. So the teacher would pick up on it in class as well and say something like, 'Sonia! You are not speaking correct English,' and can you believe it, Sonia would reply something like, 'But, Miss; it's like... well, I always talk like this don' I, you know what a mean? It's like... normal... innit?'

"She was speaking a sort of combination of a London teenager with cockney accent!"

Dorothy and Maria both simultaneously burst out laughing together.

"The whole class burst out laughing, too, and do you know what followed after this? Well we all started speaking in the same manner much to the horror of every adult, especially our parents. We had such great fun!"

Dorothy and Maria were very quickly becoming really good friends in spite of the obvious age difference between them. True, Maria was seventeen going on eighteen, though as far as maturity was concerned you could say seventeen going on twenty-one. This was probably due to the fact that she had taken much responsibility in the home over the last two years because of her dad's circumstances. She had prepared meals, washed and ironed, cleaned the house – all to the best of her ability – as well as doing a full time course of study, though the latter was slowly going down the pan as she would put it, or better still perhaps, down the chute!

It was these things, all of which were preoccupying Maria's life at this present time, that had prompted Dorothy to talk to her. There had to be a better way for her. Getting support with the cleaning and meals for her dad would help for starters, so that Maria could dedicate herself to her studies much more than she was doing at present.

Upon reaching *Max's Coffee Bar*, the two sat discussing all these matters for a good half hour. Finally, Dorothy concluded the conversation and said, "Alright then, Maria, I will enquire with social services and book a visit for someone to come and assess the situation. That will be a good start. I suspect certain parts of the care package will be free and others your dad will have to pay for, but according to what you say, he should be able to afford that with his pensions and disability allowance. Is that right?"

Maria nodded, "I'll have a word with Dad about it tonight."

"Fine; let's do it."

Having sorted out with Maria what was uppermost in Dorothy's mind, mainly Maria's welfare, she went on to discuss other things that Dorothy considered equally important, if not more so.

So often, young people spend much of their lives being talked at, talked about, and talked to, so that it can become rare for someone to simply listen to what they have to say!

Dorothy, being well aware that Maria had been going through a rough time with her dad, simply wanted to listen to her friend talk, so this she instigated by tactfully asking her if she would like to speak about herself, maybe her feelings and her ideas about life in general.

"Oh, Dot! How nice of you to ask! It makes a pleasant change to talk to someone who hasn't got just half a brain!" Maria warmed to the idea, especially as she could easily relate to Dorothy. Feeling at ease and in a safe environment to express herself, Maria spent no less than half an hour doing just that. Following on from those topics of conversation, Maria herself then instigated the next one.

"What about who I am?" grinned Maria. "What makes me, me?"

"Wow, that is a tough one!" exclaimed Dorothy. "I will have to think back about myself now. Your question is probably the one goal we both need to sus out!"

Both girls smiled at each other. It was a rare opportunity for both of them to talk in this manner, and they appeared to relish it. Dorothy considered that Maria's thoughtful question posed to her may well involve, first of all, an honest perception of what she thought about herself first.

After some thought, Dorothy realised she had to be honest and open with Maria – as indeed with herself – and so raised that major topic of concern that all young ladies share.

"How do you think you look; how do you feel about yourself?"

"There is a proverb in the Bible," Dorothy continued "that goes something like, '*As a man thinks, so he is.*' Therefore, it follows that what we think of ourselves is important!"

Maria knew this was the real deal topic! She thought about herself and her true feelings for a while, cautiously wondering just how frank she should be in answering Dorothy's question! As a consequence, her words initially seemed to be held back as if with some degree of hesitation, but then she just came straight out with it anyway.

"Teenage girls have to deal with so much pressure, you know!"

"What sort of pressure do you mean?" Dorothy had said this, not wishing to dominate the conversation herself, but rather wishing to give way for Maria to speak her own mind on the matter.

"Well, you know, all that stuff we get bombarded with – the messages we look at all the time, like you know… you see this picture of a dishy girl with awesome ultra-slim body, and so you feel you've got to look like that too. You've got to be thinner, prettier; that's the message you get all the time. What with the media, magazines, adverts in the streets, television, movies, images, then more images all thrown at you literally thousands of times in a week! Everywhere you go, wherever you lock, it's the same thing, you know what I mean?

"Sexual images, that's what they are! Of course, all the boys then go and latch on to this idea, don't they? Like, it's all about sexual imagery and all that; it's all about sex; everything trys to pressure you into looking sexy! If you want a boy, then you can bet what he's gonna want! You see it all the time in film scenes and much more on television than there used to be; nobody seems to care anymore! There's no respect! Then there's the chat rooms and internet; well...that is another story!

"Some girls are so pressured that they feel they must give in to having sex if they want a boyfriend, but in the end it never actually works like that. So many boys are not sincere; they are just out for what they can get, and the girl gets dumped afterwards! Sometimes they end up becoming really tragic cases, if you know what a mean. I've known some girls cut themselves, feeling they are worthless – or they get depression big time!"

Maria stopped for just a moment as if the things she had just spoken about were real in her own life, though it was not clear whether she herself had experienced any of them or whether she was thinking about others she knew who had!

"Awful!" exclaimed Maria. "It's, like, what boys expect now as the norm! I know someone…"

Dorothy listened intently as Maria continued more and more! She had so very much to say regarding this culture she lived in – this sexualisation of young girls and even children through images displayed every day, and the psychological demands they placed upon every single teenage girl!

Maria, at this point was displaying some measure of personal frustration and displeasure about all that she had bravely said regarding the world she lived in. Through it all, however, Dorothy had shown no shock or embarrassment, even though Maria had spoken so openly and explicitly!

This was real, straight from the horse's mouth! It was now most needful for something to be said to Maria to try and combat all this negativity she was feeling and to attempt to show her life from a different perspective to the one which consumed her thinking.

Dorothy thought how she might offer some reassurance and encouragement to Maria and felt it necessary to tell her friend just what turmoil she herself had been through as a teenager regarding the very same issues. She wanted Maria to know she was not alone.

"It was not easy; it was not fair!" Dorothy said. "But we can help one another, can we not? And since we both believe in God, we can together look to Him for help and advice, right?"

Dorothy was filled with compassion at this point, compassion for the horrible plight of her friend and all of the others too!

Oh! How important, thought Dorothy, *to have prompted Maria to speak openly like this revealing that which was upon her heart! How beneficial for Maria to confide in me without having to hear the all too familiar judgemental reproach resounding back. How many other young girls out there must feel exactly the same, but are inhibited to speak out, being too afraid to do so because they cannot really trust anyone with their intimate feelings? How are they coping with these onslaughts from what amounts to sexual image bombardment and exploitation that completely presents the wrong image of who you are and the uniqueness and beauty of what God made you to be?*

Dorothy was desirous to change the atmosphere as best as she could to one that was lighter and less dismal. Being a Christian, she always found that however great a problem or circumstance, God's Word would always give an answer, a completely different perspective upon the same matter!

She recalled from the past how she had been reading the Psalms and how she had commented to herself something like, 'I could do with some of this! If these words are relevant at all today, then they must work for me too!'

Now was such a time when the remedy of God's wisdom and truth were particularly needful! Knowing full well that Maria also loved the Lord, Dorothy felt at liberty to talk freely to her.

"Maria! That was well said! Well done! It was just awesome listening to you!"

Dorothy clapped her hands gently in applause to Maria's great speech. "You have spoken so bravely, Maria. Wow! That was literally, like, so awesome, you know!"

Upon hearing Dorothy imitating the manner in which she spoke, a smiling Maria reminded her friend a second time that she must be careful not to sound 'like a prize jerk' and that she should stick to the sphere into which she was born or words to that effect.

Nevertheless, Maria conceded somewhat this time. "No, actually, you must be careful now, Dorothy, because you are slowly, very slowly mind, beginning to sound like me just a little bit in your talking!" And she actually meant what she said.

"That's because I am listening to you so much, Maria; it's catching!"

Dorothy expressed some of her own thoughts next to follow on from all that Maria had said regarding herself and how she felt.

"The fallacy in thinking, or worse still, in believing that I am not good enough or pretty enough is shown when you look at what God's Word says about each one of us, Maria. God says we are all wonderfully and fearfully made!"

"Okay, Dot! What does *fallacy* mean?" queried Maria.

"Whoops! So sorry, Maria," exclaimed Dorothy. "A fallacy is a mistaken belief or, put simply, a lie! It is not true at all!

"It's not true if I say that I am not good enough or pretty enough! I believe everyone is beautiful to someone. Beauty is in the eye of the beholder, and everyone has some special gift from God that no one else has in quite the same way! Besides, being pretty will fade away in the same way a flower does, but not beauty; beauty is what's inside of you. It will never grow old. It will last forever!

"The truth is we are all individuals. The whole idea of us feeling a pressure or necessity to look like someone else is a contradiction to this fact. If I am trying to do that, then what I am basically doing is admitting to a lie that I am not good enough! Well, I guess God doesn't desire to make everyone the same. Look at all the flowers or trees or anything! Insects, fish, and all the animals! Are they all the same? Each one, I guess has its own unique beauty and is made perfectly! So it is with us, Maria; if you wish to know the truth about yourself, then I could tell you what I think!"

"Yeah, right!" replied Maria, "Go on then."

Replying in a humorous way, but also with sincerity, Dorothy said to Maria, "Well, to me, you are a great person, Maria! You are who you are – a pretty girl, bouncy and full of life! You are thoughtful and care about others and not just about yourself. Actually, you may not realise this, but you help me a lot by getting me out of myself. In short, there is no one else the same as you! That is a good thing, not a bad thing. It means that you have unique, special, God-given qualities and abilities that no one else has! I think that is awesome, Maria! Just look at you! You are kind and considerate. You have shown this by how you willingly help to look after your dad. You have the most wonderful personality, Maria! I feel your love and warmth whenever I am in your presence! God has made you a most wonderful person just as you are! You have good character inside of you, too. Just look at the way you spoke a moment ago! You desire something much better in life than what is thrown in your face all the time, and you show it!

"Oh, Maria, this may surprise you, but do you know I used to hate myself? Maybe I will tell you details another time, but really... I did!"

Maria simply glared at Dorothy in disbelief upon hearing what she had just said. It seemed to sum up their whole conversation.

"If that is the case," replied Maria, "Like, you of all people hating yourself... well, then we are all definitely being deluded!" exclaimed Maria. "You are so beautiful, Dorothy, and clever! It seems, like, crazy you know that you should ever have felt like that!"

"Thank you, Maria. You may never know what it means to me to hear you say that! I know what you are saying, Maria, but things are not always what they seem in life."

Dorothy showed no offence upon hearing Maria's outspokenness and implication. Maria was right! She had been deluded and now, in looking back, she knew Maria was correct, though at the time it certainly would not have seemed so.

No, Dorothy was not in any way offended; in fact, Maria's comment may just have revealed how she herself should have seen the fallacy in her own mind and way of thinking whenever she had desired to be more beautiful than she perceived herself to be. Perhaps something had just rung true; perhaps what they had been discussing had suddenly seemed to make sense and been helpful and enlightening to one another!

"Maria!" Dorothy addressed her friend in a manner that suggested she was about to propose something to her, both having finished their coffee ages ago and the conversation having run its course too.

"I fancy going to some shops to browse around. Do you feel like coming with me? I mean, there is no law that says we cannot make ourselves feel good by wearing something nice, if you get my drift?"

Maria smiled with a new found joy and excitement; after all they had both been talking about deep, meaningful stuff. What a nice surprise this was from Dorothy! They both rose from their seats, and the two of them left arm in arm.

One could hear Dorothy speaking to Maria as they departed saying, "If you will, Maria, you may choose a top or something for yourself, please, and should you wish to get any makeup or such things, feel free to do so! I will be curious though to see what you choose, and why you particularly choose it! Ha, ha!"

Chapter 14

Mary Osborne Receives a Visitor

Following her meeting with Miriam at the cafe regarding visitation, Dorothy had become very excited and for the next day or so the prospect of seeing Mary again hardly left her mind.

She had never seen or heard from Mary ever since the time they had met at *Max's*, where Dorothy had obliged her by buying her a coffee. Though they were complete strangers, such was the easiness of conversation they had shared that Dorothy had disclosed much of her personal experience to Mary.

Their conversation, it had to be said, evolved into mutual encouragement for Mary, who was also suffering from depression just as Dorothy was. However, it was true to say that other than the Petersons, no one else knew anything of Dorothy's past regarding her mental state and the severe condition that had resulted from her traumatic child abuse experiences.

Now it happened that Dorothy often took one afternoon off work, having accumulated extra hours, and today was such an occasion. Dorothy had made a phone call previously to Mary and arranged to see her at her home, and since it was in the vicinity of where Dorothy lived, she chose to walk there.

Thinking it would be nice to take a little something for Mary, Dorothy called in at a supermarket on the journey and bought some chocolate biscuits and then visited a florist to buy a bunch of colourful flowers.

Upon arrival at Mary's address, the two gave each other a hug and went indoors. Dorothy declared how amazing it was that the two of them should meet up a second time!

"It's like a miracle, dear Mary! It is so wonderful to see you again! Who would have thought that we could possibly meet like this?" They both sat down and had a coffee together, and Dorothy's biscuits came in useful.

Mary was 30 years of age. She came from a family of two, having a brother who was very close to her. Her father was a gruff, old ex-seaman of similar age to Maria's father. He had retired some four years ago and lived by himself not too far away from Mary. He had lost his wife a couple of years earlier to a severe stroke.

However, he hardly ever moved from the vicinity of his rocking chair and rarely ventured outside so that visits to his daughter were few and far between. Her brother, on the other hand, visited his sister on most days. Ever since Mary's divorce, he felt compelled to help her as much as possible, especially since she had a two year old daughter called Julia to care for.

Dorothy and Mary must have talked for well over an hour. Dorothy had much empathy and understanding for how Mary felt. She was experiencing a form of depression fairly similar to that which Dorothy herself had endured over a very long period of time. Whilst it may be true to say that all such cases of this illness are never quite the same, there are similarities which make it quite easy to understand one another's adverse feelings and emotions with this disposition. Dorothy was able to speak positively to Mary about how she had coped and how she had eventually succumbed to taking medication at the advice of Miriam Peterson. She reiterated the importance of purposely thinking positive thoughts to counteract every negative one and to learn both to relax and occupy oneself with any activity, however mundane, such as reading or knitting. Walks in the fresh air were also very beneficial. The important point was always to keep oneself occupied! All of these activities were of interest to Mary. She had a routine of taking a walk to the shops each morning and was attempting to knit her daughter a jumper.

Dorothy continued, "Why, Mary, I actually got free one-to-one counselling and attended groups with other people of similar situations to my own. These are all very good, and I do believe there are hobbies like art therapy classes too."

Mary lifted her eyes with interest at the friendly face of her visitor who clearly seemed genuine in her attempts to help her. It was so nice to talk with someone who understood her sickness! Yes, it could be said that Dorothy's visit was already proving to be beneficial to her.

"Thank you, Dorothy. I will enquire about these things. Let me go into the kitchen and make some more coffee; we are almost empty."

Whilst Mary was occupied in the kitchen, there was a gentle knock on the door and a man walked straight inside closing the door behind him.

"Hello, it's only me, David; are you there, Mary?" The visitor walked towards the lounge where they were having coffee and pushed the door ajar. He was taken very much by surprise to see someone other than Mary sitting there alone, and his eyes were immediately fastened upon the person of Dorothy, her face being exceedingly familiar to him.

"Oh! I'm sorry to intrude! I do hope this is not an inconvenience to you. I'm afraid I tend to just barge my way in to Mary's house most days. I like to check on her from time to time."

David was a fairly quiet person and normally gentle in his mannerisms. He always displayed a ring of confidence about him, which, together with those qualities previously mentioned, created an easy, free atmosphere wherever he went.

"Not at all," replied Dorothy, feeling quite at ease with his intrusion and immediately recognising him as the man she had previously met at church. Yes! He was the very same gentleman who had come over and spoken to her! She had considered him to be very pleasant indeed!

At this point Mary entered the room with more coffee.

"Hi, Davy," she said casually without any surprise whatsoever at seeing him. "This is my friend, Dorothy." Then, turning towards Dorothy, she said, "And this is my brother, David."

"I really should leave you two alone and come back later," added David not wishing to impose himself upon their time together.

"Not at all," replied Mary. "Dorothy has come to visit me for the church."

"Yes, I do believe I understand the situation very well. I was the one, Mary, who asked for a visitor on your behalf, remember? But I had no idea Miss McGuire would be that person!"

Turning again to Dorothy, David took the opportunity to address the one he held in high esteem and respect with the same air of formality as that of his sister's introduction and said, "Miss McGuire! It is you! How very nice to see you again! Yes, I did ask the pastor's wife to send a visitor to see Mary – and of all people it is you!

"Tell me, how are you now? Are you feeling any better?"

Dorothy stared at David momentarily puzzled and trying to ascertain the reason he was enquiring about her in this way, as though she had been ill or something. Not recollecting just what he was referring to, she pursued the matter no further.

However, Mary did pursue her brother's enquiry and sought to clarify for Dorothy just which situation he had been thinking about.

"I think David is referring to the occasion outside of the bowling alley during the disturbance. Were you hurt at the time, Dorothy?"

"Oh! Do you know about that occasion then?" replied Dorothy gazing at Mary, exceedingly surprised.

"Why, yes! David told me... he said... " Mary stopped. She felt it out of place to say any more, so instead allowed her brother to explain.

"Why, Miss McGuire, it appears you do not know? Is that true?"

"I'm not sure just what you mean," replied Dorothy looking totally bewildered. Seemingly, David knew things about the occasion in question of which she was oblivious.

"Miss McGuire, do you not remember how I came over to you after you had been knocked down? I phoned an ambulance for you!"

David suddenly realised that Dorothy really was unaware of all that had happened and had in no way recognised him that evening at the scene – that it was he who had come to the rescue. The truth now dawned upon all!

The revelation to Dorothy that David was the gentleman who had come upon the scene outside the bowling alley was both an embarrassment to say the least, as well as a moment requiring gratitude upon her part.

Dorothy blushed somewhat. "Thank you very much for your help, David. Maria told me that a stranger came to help. I had no idea it was you! Did you also go to help Ian at the police station?"

"Yes, I did."

"...and then drove him over to the hospital?"

"Yes. I happened to be driving back from visiting my father when I saw all the commotion outside. People were screaming and running out of the way from all of the fighting. When I pulled aside and got out of my car, I saw a lady who was hurt. Upon closer inspection I recognised you, Miss McGuire! I was aghast to see you hurt, and your friends seemed very distraught and panicky. The least I could do was call an ambulance. Hence, I asked you just now if you were any better, but... Sorry if I caught you unawares; I automatically assumed you knew."

The conversation gradually returned to where it had left off before the revelations regarding the bowling alley incident.

Dorothy had also been taken by surprise with the enlightenment that the two people in her presence were brother and sister – that David Osborne and her previous acquaintance, Mary, whom she had first met at *Max's*, were actually related! Further, the stranger who had approached her after the church service that Sunday evening was, just as she had half imagined, the same gentleman who also had spoken to Miriam requesting a visitor for his sister Mary.

"It is a small world!" said Dorothy.

Meanwhile, Mary had shown her brother to a seat and given him a cup of coffee.

"Here, David," she said passing him a plate. "Have one of Dorothy's biscuits."

"So, you two have met each other before then in fact? Upon no less than two occasions it seems!" Mary said, smiling whilst looking in the direction of her brother.

"Yes, I first spoke to Dorothy after the evening service to say how much I enjoyed her ministry – and of course the second occasion, which only I apparently knew about!"

David had felt obliged for Dorothy's sake to declare exactly what his sister had implied in her statement regarding the two occasions when both he and Dorothy had previously met, just in case she needed clarification!

Dorothy smiled warmly at David's last comment, for whilst it was true he had seen her on two occasions, she was only aware of one of them!

"Well, there's a thing," said Mary who couldn't help but notice the pleasure in her brother's eyes at meeting Dorothy again.

"Thank you, David and Mary," said Dorothy, who was now standing up ready to excuse herself.

She glanced towards David, "I am pleased you enjoyed the meeting that Sunday, David. You should come again; perhaps both of you together next time? That would be nice, Mary, if you could come too – and Julia of course. Well, I really must be going now. I have enjoyed seeing you again, Mary, and you too, David."

Mary thanked Dorothy and expressed a wish to see her again sometime soon.

Dorothy, having said her farewells again, was in the process of walking to the door when she turned her head towards David, smiled and said, "By the way, my name is Dorothy. You *may* call me Dorothy."

Secretly, Dorothy had found David's formal address to her earlier quite pleasurable. It was uncommon for someone to be so dignified in their manners, and she remembered he had also greeted her accordingly that time after the church meeting. It made her feel quite honoured and special; it demonstrated a very respectful person, and she felt good about it!

So Dorothy finally left them both, waving goodbye at their door, and afterward made straight for home.

Upon arriving at her house and opening the door, she saw a letter that was hand delivered lying upon the floor. Her usual ritual after picking up the mail was to take it upstairs to her flat, make a cup of tea, then take off her shoes and curl up on the sofa to read it.

This she did, and having taken a few sips of her camomile tea, began opening the letter. Upon reading the contents Dorothy became somewhat subdued and placed the letter down on the table next to her drink. It was from her landlord. His daughter was returning home from New Zealand and would be requiring a place to live. Dorothy had been served one month's notice to vacate her flat thus ending her tenancy!

Chapter 15

David and Mary Osborne

David Osborne could be described in all points as a gentleman. It is often noticed and commented that within a family there always seems to exist opposites in both nature and temperament.

David's father could be portrayed as a brash, rough-edged, character and though harmless enough, he often lacked some of the finer qualities in life, that is to say, in his case, politeness and sensitivity.

David, however, acted in stark contrast to his father. He was a unique individual with a wide variety of qualities. His personality was as mellow and gentle as a floating feather in a soft warm breeze, and his manner could be described as noticeably self-controlled with the patience of Job. He was so gentle as to be considered by some as weak; so kind and giving as to be easily taken for granted; so patient and long-suffering as to be irritating; and his humility was often mistaken for fragility of some form or another.

Further to this long list of attributes, David had an air of confidence about him that was to a weaker frame of mind unsettling or belittling! As a consequence he was, at large, seen but not heard, for he was never quite loud enough, though was noticed considerably whenever he did speak with a charisma that would attract long-lasting attention. He was trustworthy and reliable but did not exhibit enough daring excitement and humour to catch many female fish of the sea! Not that he had any substantial defect other than perhaps omitting to use sufficiently tempting bait!

There was always, however, a hope that one day David Osborne would meet his Miss Perfect, for he was blessed with good looks and merely awaited the right person – a person who could appreciate him and perhaps even welcome him as a pleasant change to the more sensually attractive but over-caught male fish, who initially seemed to have all the right credentials and colours but later on, over a period of time, revealed a strong lack in the essentials.

It should be said that David had an admirable quality that could prove useful in impressing the right lady, that is, if they were to ever discover it! David was a *black belt* in karate! It may well be that his dedicated training and commitment to this sport over many years had contributed to his developing a high level of confidence and not just fitness.

David was devoted to his sister. He visited her two or even three times a week to help with domestic tasks. Mostly he helped her wash up or clean the house, made a meal and sometimes collected her daughter, Julia, from school. Mary was very fortunate to have a brother like David, and she enjoyed his generosity, relishing every opportunity that he made him available to her. It was true to say, however, that Mary never took David for granted in spite of the ease with which she could have exploited his seemingly unconditional kindness towards her. Instead, she loved her brother dearly. They had always been very close when growing up as children, and this relationship had never depleted with the years – and was in fact stronger now with the current situation in which Mary found herself, looking after Julia on her own.

It was difficult at the moment for Mary to work. She had originally looked for part-time opportunities to fit in around school times, but that was before she had fallen ill with severe depression. It was not an overestimation to say that Mary currently found life quite arduous and her future was uncertain. She only managed to live on a day-to-day basis and could not cope with anything more.

David was thirty-two years of age and well established in computing. At school, his grades were not outstanding, but through resilience and perseverance he had progressed through college and then gone on to University. It was here he had developed an interest in computing, and after graduation had worked in industry and remained in the same job for eight years. His early years of struggle had been rewarded, but not without a long process of applying himself more with determination than natural ability or academic excellence.

The nature of his work required him to work independently most of the time, which did not deter him in the least, and he had progressed in the firm very well and was now a senior member of the team. It had prospered him financially too. He owned a two-bedroomed flat, drove a black convertible and was always on hand for Mary with financial assistance whenever she was in need. David had never been married, though on one occasion it was very much in his heart to be so – but without success, the other party not sharing his way of thinking regarding that ceremonial form of commitment.

David's visit to see his sister that afternoon and the unexpected meeting of her guest, Dorothy, had impacted him emotionally. Something had ignited a flame within him – a flame of new hope where previously there was none. She was going to be visiting Mary again; this pleased him very much. He found her beautiful, sincere and genteel in her manner and graces, a combination of qualities he had not seen before.

It had to be said that David no longer saw outward beauty alone as the one and only quality when looking for the right young lady. He had discovered this the hard way!

His sister observed him intently. He was still at her home and sat very quietly and thoughtfully upon an easy chair, Dorothy having left about thirty minutes earlier. She decided to interrupt his reverie with a pointed question, "David, how do you find Dorothy?"

David responded without hesitation. "Very well indeed!" he exclaimed, for he was simply thinking aloud about the very subject he had been so engaged with. Lifting his eyes and gazing at his sister he asked, "And how did you know I was thinking about her?"

"Well, I knew you were preoccupied by something, and seeing as Dorothy had not long gone, I wondered whether it was related to her in any way. Yes, she is most attractive!" agreed Mary somewhat jovially. "I thought you probably liked her, and I couldn't help but notice how you appeared to be very happy when she was here."

"You are quite right, Sister, as usual," replied David again, quite open and uninhibited to share his thoughts. "I do particularly like her; in fact, she is probably the nicest and most beautiful woman I have ever met!"

"Well now, David, you really have been hit by a thunderbolt!" said Mary smiling, very impressed by her brother's openness. "But you men are all the same; you think lovely things about a woman but never get round to saying what you really feel to her in person. I imagine

Dorothy will never get to know of these wonderful comments you have just made about her. A woman loves to hear these things, you know, even if she is not interested in the man who says them, and how many potential loves have been lost through silence and failure to disclose one's true feelings!"

Upon hearing this last comment, David chose to change the trend of the conversation. He had no intentions at this stage to commit himself to doing anything about his warm sentiments towards Dorothy; neither could he envisage for sure that at some time in the future he would do so either, but the enlightenment of Mary's frankness regarding the emotions of the female sex he kept in his heart, having been challenged to be open and honest in the future if and when the occasion should ever arise.

He went on to ask his sister, "And how is it you know her, Mary?"

In response to this question Mary got up from her chair and sat next to her brother upon the sofa, for as yet David knew nothing of her previous meeting with Dorothy at the cafe.

Mary replied, "Well, I first met Dorothy in *Max's* about three or four months ago. You remember I was not well then, David. I was having a bad time after Raymond up and left. Anyway, I was in the process of buying a coffee and then, standing there with a queue behind me, embarrassed myself realising that I did not have enough money to pay for it! Well, suddenly out of nowhere, your beautiful Dorothy appeared, offering to pay. I felt so conspicuous and embarrassed at the time! Well, she invited me over to a table to sit with her and Miriam, the pastor's wife. She was so very happy to help, really friendly I thought, and down to earth.

"Well, we both opened up to one another, and I told her my circumstances and what had just happened to me – my husband and all… having left me alone with Julia for another woman. I just came straight out with it feeling quite upset really, but I suppose at the time I needed someone to share it with. Well, Dorothy then went on to tell me some quite awful things she had experienced too."

"What sort of things?" asked David with particular interest.

"Well… they are rather personal matters," replied Mary wishing now she had not provoked David's curiosity, "and it wouldn't be right for me to say much, only that she had some very difficult times in her childhood.

"If I hadn't asked you to go to the meeting on that Sunday, I might never have seen her again. At the time, I just felt I needed a woman to talk to, you know… that's why I wanted you to ask the pastor to send someone… but I never dreamed they would send me the very same Dorothy! It is quite something!"

Upon this reflection, Mary suddenly found herself quite moved.

"Oh, how amazing is that, David?" Mary had clasped her brother's hand as the coincidence dawned upon her.

"It is indeed," replied David. "Needless to say I am glad now I responded and did what you asked, because I wasn't too comfortable about going at the time with it not being my own church. I'm pleased I went now!"

Mary simply smiled at her brother and never said another word.

Chapter 16

Dorothy Addresses her Shortcomings

The following day at work, Dorothy found it difficult to concentrate, the thought of having to move out of her flat being uppermost in her mind. She had certainly changed address several times in the past, and the experience was not new to her, but of late she had found a place to live which she called home. It was both near to her work and to church, and she had grown very fond of it having had some pleasant memories there.

The news in fact came as a shock, so much so that she wore a saddened countenance that morning as she sat in her office chair swivelling occasionally from side to side in a sentimental mood.

For the first time in a long while Dorothy had become unsettled with anxious feelings and thoughts that had opened up the vulnerable part of her. She had learned to cope with all manner of difficult situations and extremes and had a history to underline this – situations and circumstances, which in comparison were far weightier than this fairly trivial one now facing her, but she was still prone to unexpected fears and anxieties that could seem to reawaken without notice in the face of a problem where there was no immediate solution, especially in this case which was completely out of her control.

On one occasion the central heating boiler in her flat kept malfunctioning, and the engineer had been called out three times in the space of as many weeks. In spite of the fact that the boiler was covered by insurance, Dorothy had become quite paranoid about whether it was working properly and kept checking it again and again to see if it was as it should be. Her continual anxious frame of mind and seeming inability to let go of the situation triggered a panic attack when it did actually break down again unexpectedly! This led to anxiety and depression which made her feel quite ill.

Dorothy was in a state of numbness dwelling in a cave of anguish and insecurity which though entirely in her mind was very real with detrimental physical effects, and this in stark contrast to her victorious and happy day previously spent visiting Mary.

How she herself now wished someone could visit her! During her lunch break Dorothy felt the need to speak to someone, so she decided to phone Mary planning to remain composed about everything. Upon dialling Mary's number, she was unexpectedly confronted by the voice of David.

"Oh! Hello, Miss... Dorothy, how are you?" His greeting was a combination of Miss McGuire and Dorothy, but what came forth was a sort of blending of the two. Dorothy, not wishing to answer his greeting directly and rather than giving an outright false response, immediately asked to speak to Mary.

"I'm sorry, but Mary is not here. She has just gone out to collect Julia from school. Can I take a message?"

"Well, I just wanted to tell her some news, but... it can wait," said Dorothy hesitantly. "Perhaps you could just let her know that I received some unfortunate news when I arrived home yesterday. I have to vacate my flat by the end of the month, and I'm not really looking forward to moving yet again! I so liked it there."

David, not knowing the depths of what Dorothy was feeling, had nevertheless noticed a sense of disappointment and sadness in her tone of voice – something that could be considered quite sensitive coming from a man! With a desire to be as kind and helpful to Dorothy as he possibly could, he spoke reassuringly.

"I'm sure everything will work out just fine for you, Dorothy. I will look out for any vacant places and ask at work."

Dorothy thanked David and hung up. *Well, he seemed to have a positive attitude*, she thought upon finishing the conversation.

When it rains, it pours as the saying goes. So it was with Dorothy during this sudden dilemma that was preoccupying her mind.

The next level of torment was about to kick in, for a certain measure of shame and guilt regarding her very own words preached at the church meeting began to plague her with a sense of failure.

All that she had spoken about to others – namely to overcome any negative mind set with a positive attitude – could not seemingly be put into practice by her at this instant! Dorothy, at this recollection, could easily have been drawn into a self-infliction of hopelessness and reproof for not living what she preached, but instead she sought encouragement with the truth that all persons are strong in some things and weak in others.

We should not beat ourselves up about any sense of failure, especially when trying to resolve absolutely everything by ourselves, she thought.

She was sliding down the slope of despair until this ray of enlightenment had entered her soul! Instead of acting alone, she would try seeking out a person or a friend to help and support her, and perhaps pray about the matter with her.

It was not clear where Dorothy obtained this gem of sound wisdom that afternoon, but, whether by coincidence or not, it seemed to manifest itself not long after hearing the kind and reassuringly positive words from David.

Dorothy put her thoughts into action straight away.

There is someone I can think of, thought Dorothy. *I can phone Miriam!*

Dorothy went back into her work place that afternoon much happier than when she had left it. In fact, truly observant people who may have noticed her serious, sombre mood upon entering her office that morning, would have observed her now wearing a gleeful smile! A simple yet important lesson had been learned that day, namely that if in trouble, tell someone about it – someone that is who will provide their help and support!

Dorothy was in good spirits that evening as she sat upon her sofa sipping her usual camomile tea and reflecting upon the day's events. She was tired. Her body was recovering from its ordeal of anxiety, even though her mind was relieved and now free of it.

The experience was familiar. After a sort of shock or panic attack, the body would become full of adrenaline. Now, Dorothy was experiencing a kind of withdrawal, manifested in feelings of tiredness and exhaustion. The symptoms were like hot flushes passing through her, waves that caused headiness and sleepiness. During the latter few hours at work, her hyper-mood triggered by excitement and relief had produced over exuberance. She now found herself exhausted, yet with a tranquil contentment. It was an unusual combination, but she was well on the way to recovery from the blip that had happened to her upon hearing her unsettling news.

Dorothy sipped her tea, leaned her head back resting it upon a cushion, and then closed her eyes in meditation.

What a day, she thought. *I'm so glad of David's offer of help! Now I must approach the matter of moving house in a more peaceable manner and without the torment of fear!*

Where Jesus is tis Heaven there! What is my problem!? David is so funny at times! I must learn to be like that!

Her current financial outlay regarding rent and expenses had up until now been very favourable. She was close to work and within a good distance from Pastor and Miriam's home, and for that matter, was within walking distance of Mary's house.

Even now, in a place of recovered strength, the thought of losing all of these conveniences could still threaten Dorothy should she venture again down the road of negative thoughts. After all of this Dorothy was still under a potential spell that could easily have taken her back again, but it was interrupted by her sheer determination to think differently about the whole matter. Having already just experienced the dismal effects of not doing so before, she had no intention of replaying the tape again!

This sensitivity and unpredictability in her thought life was typical of her depressive condition, so that Dorothy could be fine one minute, but then overtaken the next by what could only be described as an onslaught of fear!

A more normal reaction with many people over the same matter would probably be in the form of a disappointment and a temporary feeling of regret, but nothing more. In Dorothy's case, however, it was a traumatic moment. This was the plight of Dorothy on her long road to complete recovery. Dorothy would get there; she was determined to do so!

After her short rest, Dorothy got up and reached for her mobile to phone Miriam. Miriam was very surprised with the unexpected and quite sudden news regarding Dorothy's move, so she invited her over to chat about her future plans whenever she wished to do so.

"I would really like to see you soon," said Dorothy not wishing to delay and being quite eager to seek Miriam's advice, and so it was agreed that she should come over the following day. Miriam insisted Dorothy stay for dinner, too, which was received in a most acceptable manner.

Dorothy relaxed much more that evening, now knowing that things were under control.

Chapter 17

John Has an Idea

Miriam was fast becoming like a second mother in Dorothy's eyes, and it might be said that John relished the role of being a second father very well indeed, so that his wife would often comment humorously in not so many words that he forever talked about *the child* as if she were his own daughter.

Miriam would reiterate to her husband, "You must remember, Dear, that Dorothy is a grown woman and not a child anymore, just as indeed is our daughter, Rebecca."

"Of course, of course," replied John, "and yet I guess I will always think of Becky as our little girl no matter how old she is. After all, relatively speaking, we will always have the same age difference however long we live!"

Miriam glanced at her husband in a resigned fashion indicating that she would never win on this one and willingly compromised by saying that Dorothy was without any natural parents, and a fatherly figure was an essential and all too often absent figure in a young person's life and in particular a young girl's. This Miriam knew very well from personal experience, having herself suffered the loss of her loving father whilst in her early twenties and at a time when having just finished her degree.

She would have loved to confide in him and draw upon his wise opinion on more occasions than one.

As the conversation was regarding Dorothy, Miriam chose this moment to convey to John recent news received from Dorothy the day before.

"I do have something to tell you, my Dear. Unfortunately, Dorothy has to vacate her flat within the month."

John's facial expression grew a little more concerned upon hearing his wife's disclosure, and immediately he gazed at her countenance being curious to know whether she exhibited any visible signs that this was a problem to her. He wondered himself whether Dorothy would easily take this situation in her stride or otherwise.

"As a matter of fact, I perceived some slight duress in her voice when she spoke on the phone yesterday, so I decided to invite her over tomorrow evening for dinner and see what her plans might be. I trust that this arrangement is acceptable with you, John?"

Upon hearing of Dorothy's possible adverse response to moving, John's reaction was now one of increasing concern.

"Oh what a shame!" replied John in earnest. "Why, yes; it will be good to have Dorothy round for dinner, but... it is so very important that a person so young and living on her own should..." John paused for a moment, his sentence hanging in the air incomplete, "Well, she has no family to help and has been seemingly all alone and..."

The thought of any untoward hardship upon his child was most unwelcome news, so John looked to his wife for her thoughts on the matter and any solution she might suggest.

"John! Let us not be overly concerned at this stage regarding Dorothy's wellbeing. She is a big girl, and we have a big God Who is, remember, a very present help in the time of trouble!"

Miriam knew her husband very well and could tell when he was being overly concerned or fretful about a matter, particularly when it was something or, as in this case, someone close to his heart. In such cases his mind would be prone to overreact distorting his usually very good common sense. John knew his wife's opinion and assessment was the right one regarding any matter which he found to be of a delicate nature, so that he need not be tempted into any state of anxiousness about Dorothy's predicament – and in this respect alone Miriam fulfilled her role of a helpmeet for her husband quite admirably, although she also acted as counsellor speaking words of wisdom to console her other half when necessary.

Even so, John went to bed that evening still very thoughtful, and before departing in that direction he turned to address his wife with his concluding words of the day, "Well, Dear, let us make it a matter of prayer."

The following morning arrived. It was the kind of morning when the day began with a beautiful, cloudless sky, but then slowly deteriorated with the increasing appearance of cloud as the thermals began to manifest themselves. This was so often the typical English weather pattern, when the heat of the sun was insufficient to melt away any clouds!

John had risen early, and as was his habit, was found walking in the direction of the summer house at the bottom of the garden.

Some early morning birds fluttered from nearby trees and settled upon a small stone wall near to where John was standing as if waiting for their breakfast. John gladly obliged by taking a handful of seed from a box and placing it on the wall near where the birds stood waiting. Amongst them was a robin, and being more tame and bold when compared with the sparrows, he flew and then hopped to within three feet of John. Turning his head from side to side he eyeballed John in a most remarkable way peering into his eyes as if to say thank you!

At this time of the morning, the garden air always had an invigorating, fresh aroma caused by the dew. John loved it – the quiet stillness it exhibited and the peaceful atmosphere which helped him to think clearly and meditate easily.

So often he found that the solutions to problems to be addressed that day were easily found during these moments, moments when big decisions were to be made or scrutinised.

John turned around, and sitting down upon a garden bench, he viewed the rear of the house and in particular a certain rear window beyond which was a bedroom that had been empty and unoccupied for a few years. Springing forth in his mind were recollections of past memories regarding the previous occupant of that particular bedroom.

How time flies, thought John, thinking to himself about that particular occupant, namely a certain young lady called Rebecca. His mind had rolled back the clock many years, and he imagined seeing that girl shouting out to him from an open window, 'Hello, Daddy!'

It was during this reverie of John's that a thought came into his mind, loud and very clear, *What about offering that room to a certain person who needs one?*

John had entered the garden that morning with no thought of Dorothy and her current predicament of needing a place to reside, but he left it with one!

John paused before leaving to go back in the house to see Miriam and bowed praying silently, "Let your will be done."

Upon entering the house John had prepared himself for any outcome; whatever the situation was to be, he would accept it as God's will. He had put aside his own particular opinion to that of receiving any decision that was to be made and resigned himself to accepting this decision as the right one.

This is how John was, how he lived his life having no set agenda in anything besides that of doing the Lord's will. In matters like this, he would await a confirmation.

It did not follow that John in himself had no particular thought or view about the matter. In fact, the truth was he would love the thought of having Dorothy stay with them, at least until such time as when she could find a place of her own; but being who he was, he chose to be willing to sacrifice his own wishes if necessary just in case, for some unknown reason that he could not possibly foresee at this moment in time, it would not prove to be the best way forward. No, if this was to be, it had to have God's blessing upon it or it was not to be entertained. His faith was such that he expected the right decision to be made one way or another.

It was a matter of such importance that he would immediately confer with Miriam regarding his suggestion. She needed to know and be allowed to present her own views. He was very familiar from past experience that he had not always thought things through, but Miriam would certainly bring that to light if it was necessary!

"What do you think of the idea?" John asked his wife, whom he found sitting in the kitchen eating toast. Miriam was of a similar mind to her husband in major decisions, being quite wise and thoughtful too. She, however, was the last port of call. This question of John's definitely required a woman's touch.

"John, I am very happy for this to happen. I know you must have thought much about it on your part. I guess she could stay in Rebecca's room for just as long as she pleases, though I imagine she will want a place of her own in the longer term. What a thought!" exclaimed Miriam showing both surprise and excitement at the proposal.

"I have prayed about it," said John "and if you agree, then I believe it will be the right thing to do."

"I do! I certainly do!" replied Miriam. "Of course, my dear, what remains now is Dorothy's reaction to our proposal and the answer to that will soon become made known."

Miriam remembered that Dorothy had been invited over for dinner that very evening, and she had things to do. She tended, on such occasions, to cook the dinner in the morning then warm it up in the evening, this being the convenient way of organising her day.

Dorothy arrived promptly at the Petersons that evening and immediately felt the warmth of their presence as she entered. The meal that Miriam had prepared was in fact a curry dish, which actually tasted better after reheating than perhaps if it had been eaten straight away! Some meals were like that, and this was one of them. Dorothy was full of appreciation for what was now the second dinner she had partaken of in their home in as many weeks.

Meanwhile, both Miriam and John kept their composure and enthusiasm under control in a most remarkable way! Nothing regarding a certain matter in hand had been brought into the conversation thus far, and the responsibility of conveying the essence of it was designated by Miriam to her husband John.

And so it was, when dinner had finished and they were all relaxing, Miriam enquired of Dorothy's circumstances and her intentions regarding finding alternative accommodation. Dorothy declared that nothing definite had materialised as yet; it was all too soon, but she mentioned that she would look around and added that David was also looking out for her at his work.

It did not take a mind reader to understand that this subject was of concern to Dorothy, and Miriam prompted her husband that this would be an appropriate moment for him to speak.

John immediately responded addressing the lady in question. "You know, Dorothy, our daughter, Rebecca, moved into her new marital home several years ago. Well, she probably had the largest room in the house and also an adjacent smaller room which she used for her computer, and both these rooms are completely vacant to this very day! Miriam and I would like to offer you the use of our daughter's old bedroom and study and invite you to live here in this home with us for as long as you wish to, if that is you would be interested."

Now such a proposal may not have been so straight forward with any other young person of Dorothy's age, for the majority by far would desire a place by themselves providing for all the freedom and independence that goes with it. In Dorothy's situation, however, she did not feel the overpowering necessity to prove anything to herself. She had proved life for so long as an independent party living alone, and this was not necessarily a priority to her any more. She had been through that experience when she was a lot younger, and now it was like water under the bridge to her. The thought of a warm, centrally-heated room; the contemplation of more curry dishes like the one just eaten; and homemade cakes and apple pie and the like! In a nutshell, the kind of things that happen in a normal family home – of which she had little experience! She had fended for herself most of her life, not the least when having to go to boarding school.

Independence? Thank you, but...no thank you! Let that come again later; this will do absolutely fine for now! These were her thoughts and that finalised the matter.

Her mind was made up. John had made the proposal to her in such a gracious manner that she felt it right to accept the offer from Miriam and John, showing the gratitude it deserved.

"I would be delighted to do so! Thank you both so very much!"

Chapter 18

Mary's Prank

Dorothy's mind was now at rest. Things were not as she would have imagined, but what of it! She had been offered accommodation which at the end of the day was tasteful and most agreeable.

The following morning when she had woken up to go to work, she faced the day with complete peace. Now, it was in God's hands, and He had opened up a door for her. All worry and anxiety had gone out of the window as it were; this she believed was God's will. Why should she worry?

I will learn to trust God in future! Look what He has done for me! Whenever the fear of the unknown arises, I will think of Him and His Word instead of forgetting Him!

What was actually happening to Dorothy was the beginning of a new learning curve to put her trust in God! It was not easy for her, but this was what she believed. She had to learn to walk with God – and that by faith and trust alone. The Scripture coming straight into her mind that morning going to work was this:

We walk by faith and not by sight!

Dorothy had been through the wilderness, and like a Caleb spirit had come through on the other side, but there was a lot of new territory ahead which she had yet to conquer!

Friday came along very quickly. It was that time of the week when Dorothy finished work early; it was about 3pm.

As she walked towards her flat, she passed by a familiar road, and glancing at the street sign she observed the name of it as Walpole Road.

Ah yes, thought Dorothy, *I know someone who lives at number forty-six! I wonder, shall I pay her a spontaneous visit?* The answer to the proposition just relayed through her mind was always going to be yes!

Dorothy stood outside number 46 and rang the bell. Initially it appeared that no one was at home, but Mary Osborne having just entered the hallway herself was busy seeing to little Julia, who was crying. They had both just returned home from nursery school, and Julia was objecting to being taken out of her pushchair having been woken up from sleep!

Upon hearing the crying, Dorothy waited patiently until the door opened. Finally, the door swung ajar, and both ladies confronted one another.

"Dorothy! Hello! How are you?" Mary was exceedingly pleased to see Dorothy's face before her eyes – and all unplanned and unexpected.

"I am quite well, thank you," replied Dorothy just entering in and then immediately engaging with Julia who had stopped crying to observe the visitor. "I hope this is alright… to call like this. I was passing by on my way home from work."

"Of course it is! I love surprises! Would you like to take Julia for me, whilst I carry in a bit of shopping?"

Upon entering the lounge they were both taken by surprise, for judging by all the banging noise coming from that direction, someone appeared to be working in the bathroom.

"Is that you, Mary?" sounded the familiar voice of David.

"Yes! It's me. What are you doing?"

Mary was busy unpacking her groceries in the kitchen and had not ventured into the bathroom to see her brother. Consequently the conversation that was in progress continued from two separate rooms.

"I'm trying to fix that new mixer tap for you in the bathroom. What a job! How is Julia? Are you both alright?"

"Yes, we're fine. I'm just unpacking some shopping. Having sausages and mash and peas tonight, if that is alright?"

"Excellent! That'll be great, with gravy please. Thank you. When is that Dorothy coming round again to see you?"

With this unexpected turn of events in the current discourse between the two people, Mary, wearing a cheeky smile, turned around and gestured to Dorothy to be quiet by placing a finger over her lips.

"Shush!" she said smugly. "Don't say a word!"

"Why do you wish to know that?" Mary asked David in a mischievous fashion.

"Just asking, that's all."

.   " Are you sure that's all you're doing?"

"Mary! Why are you prying? You know I like Dorothy; you've already fathomed that much with your woman's intuition, so I don't quite see just why you are trying to search me out for something you already know. I don't mind reiterating again to you that I do think she is a lovely girl, and it would be nice to see her again; that's all. Are you satisfied now?"

"Well, David, I have some good news for you. Dorothy is here with me now!"

"What!" exclaimed David.

After this outburst of surprise from David, there immediately followed a bumping sound, and he could be heard crying out in pain. Upon hearing this, Mary ran straight into the bathroom to find her brother holding his head. "What have you done, David? Are you alright?"

"I banged my head, didn't I?"

Mary soothed David's head tenderly with a cold flannel and asked him again if he would be alright.

"Yes, thank you, Mary; I will be fine. Just let me come in and sit down a minute. You couldn't make us a strong coffee, could you?"

"Of course, David, please forgive me for my little prank. You know it was only a joke. Just go through and say hello to Dorothy, and I'll bring you some coffee." Needless to say, David looked daggers at his sister as he walked passed her into the lounge, so with a change of mind Mary decided in fairness to escort her brother to meet Dorothy.

As one pair of eyes met another, Dorothy could only place both hands over her face for a moment in utter embarrassment. It was the kind of mortification that had neither shame nor displeasure; it was a pleasant experience for Dorothy to have heard such authentic compliments made about her in such unusual circumstances! She smiled at David sympathetically whilst also blushing profusely.

This particular frequent occurrence of Dorothy's complexion changing to a crimson red had fascinated David! So much so that he determined in his mind from that time onwards to make the phenomenon a matter of investigation, for it had raised hope within him that it just might possibly imply that Dorothy had blushed because she had a liking towards him too! Well, this was a good line to follow – or so he thought!

David knew that the prank had been Mary's idea alone, and in this respect David appreciated Dorothy's warm and sympathetic mannerisms towards him regarding his misfortune – blushing and all!

Like most men David had need of some sympathy from a woman under these unfortunate circumstances where pain was concerned, and he couldn't have asked for a more appropriate person to give it. He also felt very embarrassed to say the least – perhaps even more so than Dorothy – but he had an added extra thrown in on his part, that of feeling rather stupid as well!

David, having chastised his sister for her surreptitious and mischievous behaviour, had by now sat down opposite Dorothy, and slowly he began to see the funny side of things too!

"Go on!" David blurted out. "Have a good laugh, Mary, before you strain your throat muscles!"

At this invitation both ladies burst out laughing, though it had to be said that Dorothy tried her very best to conceal it. Mary on the other hand struggled to control herself from being quite hysterical!

Coffee was eventually served and things got back to a more comfortable atmosphere as two certain people in particular had now resorted to civilised conversation with one another, much to the gratification of their guest.

Whilst Dorothy had never quite experienced such jovial pranks before and whilst it had been an embarrassment to her, nevertheless she would probably never ever forget the happenings of that afternoon as long as she lived. So often the small, simple and relatively insignificant moments in life hold the most precious memories, and this would certainly be one of them!

Now, as it happened Dorothy wished to ask something of David, but she was holding her ground awaiting the best and most convenient moment to do so.

Then the moment arrived. Mary suddenly became preoccupied with Julia, who up until that moment had been playing very nicely and independently, but she was getting tired and needed mummy's attention.

"David, I would like to thank you for your encouraging words over the phone the other day. I was in a bit of a quandary wondering just what to do about getting another place, and your positive attitude, I must tell you, was very reassuring to hear at that particular time. Thank you."

"Whatever I may have said, Dorothy – and to be honest I can't remember exactly just what I said – you are more than welcome. I'm pleased that you have got a place! Mary tells me that you will be staying at the pastor's house, is that right?"

"Yes. It is very convenient for me at this time until I find another place and save up enough money for a deposit, which brings me to say… would you be able to do me a great favour?"

At this point, just like a knight in shining armour, David would have gladly offered his financial help to Dorothy and may even have offered her a blank cheque if this was what she was intimating, but disappointingly money was not the nature of Dorothy's request.

"I wonder, would you possibly be able to help me move house on Saturday?"

"No problem. That'll be fine. I am totally free to help." If there had been anything written upon David's calendar for the weekend, then it just been altered!

"Oh, that is such a relief! Pastor John will be away for the day, and I did not know who else to ask. You have just saved my life! Thank you for a second time. You are a useful friend to have; I shall, as they say, owe you one! Two other young people from church, Ian and Maria, will also be helping, but I needed… how shall I say it… a man!"

"Dorothy, you just got yourself a man by the name of David! I'm at your disposal."

Dorothy, being quite a sensitive person, had feelings and emotions close to the surface, and David's last words had triggered that inconvenient, embarrassing impediment of hers which had once again sprung to life. She couldn't help herself; she blushed for the second time in the space of no less than twenty minutes!

David, as a consequence, was all the more determined to do his research!

Chapter 19

Moving House

When a statement is open to more than one interpretation, there usually follows great humour and comeback, and though the intended meaning may well be clear and fully understood by all, nevertheless what becomes highlighted and emphasised is always that meaning which was not intended!

Dorothy had just experienced a classic example of such ambiguity. She had spoken to David quite innocently, even verging on naively, when stating that she needed a man, not realising at that instant just how funny it sounded.

David was aware of this ambiguity and that it had humorous ramifications. His reply that *he was her man* was said purposely and with the intention of furthering the humour. He laughed without any embarrassment whatsoever, but Dorothy was clearly somewhat more reserved, judging by her sudden change of countenance to that of a more crimson colour yet again.

Dorothy was still vulnerable regarding any verbal expression of feeling or emotion whether spoken of in a humorous manner or otherwise.

On such occasions as these, whenever they should unexpectedly arise, she would no doubt eventually learn that a little frivolity is absolutely fine, and that it is when we take ourselves too seriously that we need to worry! Humour was important; it always helped defuse awkward situations!

Light-heartedness clearly would have helped in that brief moment of embarrassment Had Dorothy replied something to the effect, *Yes David, I do need a man; just to carry the boxes if you please! That will suffice perfectly; thank you very much for your offer;* had she demonstrated a sense of humour about the situation, everything would have been fine, for after all, it was funny!

Dorothy's circumstances regarding her childhood were not ideal in preparing her for a relationship later on in life! How impractical it can be therefore in the real world to attempt to prescribe qualifications as to what one person should be like in order to please another! Textbook advice would seem too far remote from reality in such cases as these. Was it Dorothy's fault that she was like she was? Was it David's fault for being too frivolous? In reality, two people are randomly drawn together – warts and all – and is it not what they make of it together that really counts in the end, not how wonderfully suited they were considered to be at the very beginning of their relationship?

Compatibility of faith is considered a key factor in relationships, and fortunately all three people concerned where united by their common, Christian faith in God – or to be more precise, it should be said that at this particular moment in time two were united by their faith. David was challenged by it, he being more a religious follower rather than a born-again believer like his sister and Dorothy. It had to be said that the two ladies were as different as chalk and cheese regarding Christian matters when compared with David!

So often it is one's religious upbringing that can prove to be inflexible, not because of substantial differences in the essentials but rather in the manner and degree in which faith is received, believed and appropriated.

Dorothy was a new Christian in the Biblical sense of being born again; David was an old Christian but was not born again.

Would there be a clash because of this?

Where a common faith exists between the two parties, it is considered more likely for those couples in relationships to adhere to the unselfish requirement of God's love as revealed in His written Word, where the emphasis is never exclusively upon that which one individual may desire but also upon the needs of the other party.

In such cases it may be possible, perhaps even desirable, for two people who have that mutual and essential sparkle of attraction towards one another to begin their relationship by learning of one another's differences over time and being prepared to iron out any undesirable or even contentious ones in a mutually acceptable Biblical manner – and in so doing become honest, intimate and trustworthy friends in whom they can each confide, for it is only when God's Word is equally received in love with obedience by both parties as the higher authority that they can move on together through the problems and disputes of life that are common to all!

Dorothy's difficulty with the conversation with David and the humorous ambiguity that had occurred was her inability to cope with it in the light-hearted manner required.

Was this to be the end of the line as far as David's desire for a closer friendship with Dorothy was concerned? After all, it could be considered that her sense of humour was lacking and without that essential ingredient they were never going to be compatible!

No, David had not thought this a priority, even though he knew of many people who would disagree with him, and he had clearly shown a desire to work on their differences in personality. If David really liked Dorothy as a person and not just for her outward appearance and the chemistry between them, anything was capable of being developed to the good, though it went without saying that there was not a thing to be improved in Dorothy's physical appearance or desirability as far as that was concerned.

Dorothy was not in any way perturbed, just a little uncomfortable, not knowing how to deal with the situation she faced with David; she was unaccustomed to frivolity and just needed to get used to it. David on the other hand, after his laughter had subsided, was very polite and courteous with Dorothy and did not make any more of the matter – which did relieve her just a little!

The moving day had arrived. A medium-sized, white hire van could be seen approaching Dorothy's current home, followed by a bright red car. The van stopped and reversed into a spot that was fairly close to the door whilst the red car parked on the opposite side of the road.

David got out of the van, and Ian McPherson and Maria Townsend got out of the car.

David recognised Ian straight away as the young man who had required his assistance at the bowling alley evening! They were both surprised and pleased to meet one another a second time. Likewise, Maria went over to speak with David to thank him for helping Ian on that same evening. It had been especially traumatic for her, and if it hadn't been for David's help at the police station, things could have taken a substantial turn for the worse – for Ian that is!

Dorothy took Maria to her bedroom to take clothing items and directed the two men to take the heavily packed boxes standing in the hallway. These had been packed the night before with the kind help of George, her neighbour.

"What's she got in here?" exclaimed Ian finding a particular box very heavy.

"Better we don't know, Ian!" replied David. "Actually, it feels like books maybe."

"She's a very beautiful woman, isn't she?" This was Ian's expressed feeling to David regarding Dorothy, it being a typical point of conversation and comment between two men regarding those ladies who happened to be within their company. It seemed as if it was necessary to manifest opinions in such circumstances whether good or bad – it was an unwritten law - and this time, in Dorothy's case, it was an obvious conclusion but nevertheless needed to be aired openly. That's the way it was. Consequently, it now became David's turn to pass comment upon Maria to Ian, and they both agreed unanimously; Maria was just simply a great and pretty girl!

After about two hours the removal men and ladies had finished their work. Miriam was receiving goods at her end, and the three ladies stayed to assemble all of the absolutely essential things for Dorothy. At least she had clothes to wear, a sofa and chairs to sit on, and a bed to sleep on!

After all was done, David made a suggestion to the three of them, "How would you like to go for a meal – all of you? My shout?"

"Brilliant idea," chirped Ian showing great interest; he was sitting upon some steps looking tired and hungry, and judging by his spontaneous reaction to David's invitation, his answer was a definite yes!

"Yes, I'm game also," replied Maria, who automatically echoed Ian's choice, irrespective of whether she was hungry or not. But I do need to be back home by six to get some shopping in for Dad; you're taking me, right?"

This request or perhaps instruction from Maria was aimed at Ian, looking him directly in the eye as she made it. Ian simply nodded with approval. Would he challenge her for being presumptuous and bossy towards him? No, not Ian; he never said a word.

Maria knew Ian, and Ian knew Maria; this was their mutual understanding of one another each knowing the other's ways and mannerisms. To many it may not have been acceptable, but they were just fine with one another.

Weekends were a little different to weekdays, when Alfred always had home-help and meals on wheels. Maria was very happy to help out, but she always made it fit into her social life – what there was of it. Though having said that, David's invite was outside the box, not having been planned previously, so Maria needed to work around this arrangement.

"Are you sure?" said Dorothy in response to David's invite of a free meal.

"Yes, I am sure! So that settles it then. Where would you like to go?"

After a short interaction, mainly between Ian and Maria and then finally with Dorothy, they decided to go for an Indian meal at a renowned restaurant.

The meal was served in several dishes upon a round revolving table, and they could all share each dish by spinning the table round!

"It's really great to see you again, David. I kind of really appreciated your help on that night, you know!" Ian had taken this informal occasion to thank David, who then went on to tell Ian of a similar experience in his own life.

"Not a problem. You know, Ian, too many people are automatically blamed for something that they haven't done. It happened to me once when I was about your age or a bit younger."

David, on such occasions as this where he was conversing with a young person, always sought to accommodate their comfort zone by being friendly and as frank as possible in the manner in which he spoke to them.

"I was in this grocery shop, right, and this lad was shoplifting, you know what I mean? Well, he didn't pull it off. The shop keeper was far too sharp for him. He saw what was going on, stopped the guy, and an almighty scuffle followed. Of course, I was just standing there in the queue and decided to join in, didn't I?

"Before too long the police came and took me away for questioning, as well as the guy who was responsible. The shopkeeper didn't tell the police that I was helping, did he? Until he was called upon later to verify exactly what had happened. Eventually, he came to rescue me just like I did with you, Ian!"

Ian appreciated this discourse with a much older man like David. David was not patronising and spoke to him as his equal. It was encouraging to Ian that someone else had experienced a similar thing to what had happened to him that night. It made him feel less stupid. Appearances were probably ninety percent of everything at his age. It had bothered him to have been called a prize jerk by some of his mates for stepping into the fight at the bowling alley and getting involved in the first place.

David had taken on board the responsibility of ordering, and so he asked everyone what they would like for their first course.

"Vegetable samosas, please."

"Same here."

"Onion bhajis for me."

"Can you ask if they do cauliflower and spinach pakoras, please?"

The wheels were now set in motion. Drinks came first, and everyone was talking to at least one person so that no one was left out. As it happened the pakoras were a favourite, and Maria observed them diminishing very quickly.

"Ian, save some pakoras for someone else, please," she said as Ian took the last one.

"Whoops! Sorry, Maria. Here, you can have mine; I've only had one bite."

David intervened and ordered some more pakoras to the delight of Maria.

"Thank you, David," she replied.

Ian had been talking to Maria and Dorothy when something came into his head out of the blue. Looking towards David, who was seated diametrically opposite him, he called upon his attention for he wished to ask him something.

"David, a friend of mine told me that he thinks he has seen you before." The particular friend in question was part of the group that had been tenpin bowling, and he had seen David when he had come on the scene to call an ambulance for Dorothy.

"He goes to karate lessons every Tuesday night. Are you by any chance an instructor at the karate centre down town?" enquired Ian.

"What is your friend's name?" enquired David.

At this point every tongue had ceased, and all eyes were centred upon David.

"John Tyndale," answered Ian.

"Oh yes! I know the lad. He is on his green belt, but he's not in my class. Yes! To answer your question, I do instruct at the karate centre."

Suddenly all conversation took the form of questions to David, who now found himself in the limelight. Dorothy in particular was very surprised, so much so that her impediment kicked in momentarily – though not a crimson red colour as before. She went on to ask of David what belt he was on.

"Black belt, second dan," was his reply.

"What sort of level is that?" enquired Maria.

"It's like, the top level; isn't it, David?" commented Ian.

"It's in the top group of black belts," confirmed David. In this respect David was being modest, for there were four different black belts in karate, and he was just one level below the highest!

Like most people the group imagined karate was all about inflicting punishment upon would be assailants with a karate chop or something of that nature, but David reassured them that this was not the case.

"Karate is not really like that. It is not an aggressive sport. It is essentially of course a means of self-defence. You are trained to be a peaceable and responsible person with humility, not aggressive by any means. Actually, the reason I took it up several years ago was to build up my confidence and self-esteem. The discipline did this for me; it was what I needed in my life."

Once again, Maria's vocabulary was found wanting. Turning aside to Dorothy, who sat to her left, she whispered, "Hey, Dot, what does humility mean?"

Dorothy checked it out on google with Maria's mobile and said, "Look! It says having a low view of your own importance, but in the Bible I know that it's more to do with lowliness of mind, gentleness and being submissive, like when Jesus humbled Himself."

"So, I guess if you are humble, then you are not big-headed right?" replied Maria, not entirely satisfied with the dictionary's meaning and searching for a more practical definition.

"Certainly not, Maria," said Dorothy, smiling and touched by her simplicity. "And you could add that such a person isn't bossy either or at least doesn't push hard to get his or her own way!"

"Mm, I think Ian is a little bit humble then," concluded Maria having seemingly thought of him straight away upon hearing Dorothy's simpler definition of the word.

The ladies chit-chat of a sort came abruptly to an end as Ian reminded Maria of the time.

"It's time to be going, Maria, if you need to be home by six." Maria grabbed her coat and got up to leave.

After all of the hugs and thanks, the pair went on their mission to get the shopping for Alfred, leaving David and Dorothy alone together.

Chapter 20

Two Meaningful Discourses

Within a quiet, still room an elderly man with a limp struggled to reach for a book from a bookshelf; then, he made his way back to his easy chair which, it may be said, rarely ever went cold through having no occupant seated upon it. As a matter of fact, he and that chair were like a composite body for at least six hours a day, or put more simply, the two together were like one single object.

The place where the old man sat resembled a bed-sitting room. It had a small kitchenette in one corner and a sofa that looked as though it was slept upon, for it had some blankets strewn in an untidy manner to one side; in short, he lived, ate and slept there!

He browsed through the book as if looking for a particular page and then became consumed with reading it for a good half an hour, when suddenly he stopped reading and looked up with an expression of bewilderment and surprise. He had just been reading a sentence that said, *My God, My God why have You forsaken Me?*

He put the book down, and then sat in his chair. Leaning his head right back to rest it, he began to think about what he had just read.

Shortly, he heard the sound of a key turning in the lock on the front door. A young lady and a young man entered carrying several bags of shopping.

"Hi, Dad," said Maria, followed by Ian. They both entered the cosy room and habitat of Alfred Townsend.

He ceased from his meditations over a certain reading that had been preoccupying him and placed his Bible onto a coffee table next to him in order to greet his daughter and her boyfriend.

"Hey, you two, how did yer get on then?"

"It was good, Dad… excellent! After we'd all finished, David took us out to an Indian restaurant. It was like, really bril."

"Yeah, and guess what?" followed Ian, equally pleased with the occasion. "David is a black belt instructor!"

"Who's David, I ask?" enquired Alfred.

"He's the same man who helped us all outside the bowling alley and got me out of the police station; he knows Dorothy."

"Aar… that women, aye, the one who come here wi' you, Maria, that time? That goes to yer church?"

"You have met Dorothy before then, have you? What do you think of her, Mr Townsend?"

"I know what's yeh want me to say about her, and she is that! But she can't half talk, she can!"

Maria, recognising the nature of the book that was lying upon the table next to her dad's chair, went on to comment with great surprise.

"Dad, have you been reading your Bible then?"

"Well… yeah! No law against that, is there? But I must say I got quite confused. Maybe you two can help me."

Alfred's mellow tone of voice and sudden apparent interest in reading the Bible completely astonished both Maria and Ian; it was most unprecedented. There was never a time when they had seen him doing so before.

Alfred showed his daughter the passage he had been reading, and she came alongside him and sat on the arm of his chair.

"I were reading about Jesus being crucified yeh know, but this bit I couldn't figure out. He cries out sayin' to His father, 'Why have you forsaken Me?' How's that, if He is His father? Why would He do that to Him?"

Maria was challenged by this simple and extremely important question and pondered it herself for a while.

Ian interrupted them both and spoke the first thoughts that came to mind, "Well, it's because he was taking away our sin, and God couldn't look upon sin. He was dying for our sin."

"Not sure I get that, Ian," replied Alfred.

Meanwhile, Maria had gone up to her room and fetched a small booklet that showed you how to lead someone to Christ.

"Here it is, Dad. There are Bible verses here that tell you something about why Jesus died on the cross."

Maria held the booklet before him to read.

All have sinned and fall short of the Glory of God.

All we like sheep have gone astray; we have turned everyone to his own way and the Lord has laid on Him the sins of us all.

He made Him, who knew no sin, to be sin for us that we might become the righteousness of God in Him.

"I think I gets the picture; He being punished instead of us, hey? Where did yeh get those verses from Maria? Are they out of the Bible? You'd better show me sometime how to find 'em, so I can read 'em for meself.

"I like the bit about them sheep! They don't half get lost if yeh don't watch 'em! Somebody knows what they're talking about!

"Leave that book yeh got wi' me, will yeh, Maria? I can look at it tonight."

"Of course, Dad. I'll leave it on your table, alright?"

Maria was still in shock! Her dad was being very receptive to hearing and reading the Bible, open and honest like a child! Where was this coming from, and just what had started it?

"Ian, for goodness sake sit down, Lad!" Alfred spoke in a manner that carried warmth and not harshness as it might have seemed. A person listening in another room would hear the words but could not know the manner in which they were delivered; in fact, Alfred, in his own rough manner, was being friendly and welcoming though some would surely judge that he was perhaps a little patronising and brash as well!

"Maria, make us all a cuppa will yeh? I'm very pleased yeh both come round to see me tonight. God bless yeh both."

Alfred went on, happy to talk about everything and anything, and the three had a long and pleasant conversation which, together with his reception of the Scriptures, was the second unusual event that evening.

Meanwhile, in the Indian restaurant, Dorothy and David were still seated together – though to be precise, they had now moved to a drinks area and were sitting upon comfortable sofas in an area put aside for those waiting for a table.

For over an hour, they talked to each other openly about themselves and their pasts, including some disclosed revelations regarding Dorothy and her life as a child – all of which had astounded a surprised and shocked David.

This was the only time that David and Dorothy had been alone together to talk. Their conversations in the past had always been in the presence of someone else and therefore had carried an air of formality or restriction about them, because someone else was hearing what they said. In the situation they found themselves that evening, each one could learn more about the other. Now, they had no cloak to hide behind. Their manner of speaking was open, frank, and consequently more informative to each other.

The topics of conversation moved on to deeper thing – those matters of substance and of a more personal nature regarding each other's views upon life.

"What would you like to do with your life, David? I mean, do you have any plans at all?"

"I was looking to settle down once… get married… have say… a couple of children, but that didn't work out as I told you earlier. She was not interested in a marriage commitment or children for that matter. I am thirty-two now and would like to be able to play with my kids whilst I'm still young!"

"I also think family life is so very important." Dorothy concurred.

Indeed, Dorothy had obvious reasons for saying that. "I also believe that being married is the best thing; certainly, I now know it to be God's way."

David was thinking about a matter regarding Dorothy and the attitude she always seemed to have regarding her faith in God. He had noticed this about her earlier on in their friendship, but it was only now that things came to a head and he felt it necessary to air his feelings openly.

David's dilemma was this: Dorothy seemed to him as if she had no mind of her own at times and kept referring to God's way or God's will all of the time. The truth was that he would probably find this way of life an infringement upon his liberties and freedom, so that his pride became hostile to it! David had not entered that realm of personal stuff like Dorothy seemed to have done but had been brought up in a more religious way, that is, one of regular church going and moral well-being; but it was not the same for Dorothy. With her it seemed far more personal, like she professed to know God in a real way or something of that nature! Consequently, whenever Dorothy spoke in such a personal way about God's will and His purpose for her life, David could not relate to it. It was foreign to him and ventured upon becoming annoying! They had two different mindsets.

David had been brought up in traditional church services that were composed of sombre hymn singing with organ music, formal liturgy in the Christian prayers and preaching that rarely focused upon Bible teaching and the Gospel. He had developed beliefs and accepted conventions without really thinking about them too seriously or for that matter without believing them, for they had made little impression upon his heart. In part this was probably because he had never really understood what was preached and had never been challenged in a personal way. So often the sermons were about current affairs and social matters and even politics, most of which never inspired him. Whilst he had not particularly disagreed with Dorothy regarding any doctrinal matters, he had not responded and benefited from his church experience like Dorothy seemed to have done!

In a nutshell, he had grown into the habit of paying lip-service and nothing more than that; he was a church goer but in body only, his mind and heart being quite dead to it all. He had grown accustomed to religious duties but anything different to that style and form of worship in which he was familiar was not received favourably. It impinged upon his personal lifestyle. It was an affront to that to which he was accustomed; any changes to this were looked upon in a hostile and arrogant manner.

Dorothy was different! She had seemingly brought a fresh personal relationship with God – and not merely church attendance – into the equation. All this had happened to her within the last four to five months; she had learned and received so much from the Scriptures with joy and passion, all in such a short time!

What then was the real difference between David and Dorothy? How could it be possible for one person to attend church for so many years and still not come away with a living reality of God in their life? And for another just like Dorothy to acquire such in a mere few months?

Now, David was of the same mind as Dorothy about many things. They had both shared their individual preferences regarding family, children and marriage, but David's opinion was his own with or without God being in the picture. His choice was of himself and the way he would wish to go. It had nothing to do with God's way in his eyes at all.

In a nutshell Dorothy's perception of God impinged too closely on what he considered to be his own personal freedom, his will and his rights and choices. This he could not understand of her, and to be truthful he wasn't too keen on going down that road either!

"What are you thinking about, David?" enquired Dorothy, perceiving that he was preoccupied with some matter which had all the appearances of being a problem. Of course Dorothy was spot on regarding her intuition and sensed the change of atmosphere very well indeed.

David felt compelled to be honest with Dorothy regarding the personal question she had posed to him. It was beneath him to be false or otherwise. As a consequence he went on to reiterate all of his concerns regarding the matters that were upon his heart, or certainly on his mind, and she listened attentively to what he had to say without emotion.

Within the space of half an hour, whilst mostly listening to David's discourse, Dorothy was feeling quite ill.

"I am fully aware, David, of your opinion. You have made it very clear to me in a harsh, critical and arrogant fashion and have belittled me in the process! I would like to go home now. Please would you take me home?"

Chapter 21

A Miracle

The following morning had arrived; it was quite early – 7.30 to be precise. The sky was a beautiful blue but the air chilly. The streets were very quiet with it being a Sunday and full of parked cars, for few of the owners were going to work. For many, it was the opportunity to rest a little longer in bed, though there were a few exceptions.

Some of the exceptions could be seen in a nearby field where people walked their dogs. Across this field in the far distance hung a thin blanket of mist suspended above the ground in an eerie fashion, and the grass glistened in the sunlight suggesting it was probably soaking wet with early morning dew.

It was that time of the year, late September, when an Indian summer brought beautiful sunshine in the daytime, but as the evenings drew close the temperature would rapidly drop bringing frost in the rural areas. The particular scene in question was on the edge of the suburban area coming out of town where it steadily diminished into rural so that it was cold enough for the fog to come down with a light frost.

A few other people were waiting at bus stops travelling who knows where. It was always the case that whilst most people relaxed in their home at the end of a working week, there would also be those who for whatever reason, needed to be out and about quite early – even on a Sunday morning.

Dorothy, peeping out of her bedroom window, still in her pyjamas, was observing the scene in question. She was of course now in residence at her new home, where she had her own very large bed-sitting room and a separate study room; other facilities she shared with the Petersons in their family house.

The central heating had kicked in, and already she felt the heat of the radiator for she was leaning against it! Pastor John was of the opinion to leave the boiler on all of the time and control the temperature from an external thermostat. When going to bed he would always remember to turn it down to 16-17 degrees Celsius.

I don't want the temperature to get lower than that; if it comes on, so be it.

This was his method of ensuring the house never got too cold, for he thought it would take a lot more heat to warm it up again if it did.

Dorothy sat upon her bed and read a portion out of the Bible.

... And we know that all things work together for good to those who love God, to those who are the called according to His purpose.

She then bowed her head and prayed about recent events, the good and the bad.

She was very pleased and grateful for her new place, but the previous day had ended on a sad and hurtful note for her. David had made very clear his unchanging opinion regarding certain personal matters about his religion, which though Christian, nevertheless conflicted as far as he was concerned with this newly-found, simple faith of Dorothy's. Not that he had specified any substantial differences of belief; he had just declared to her that he had his religion, and that he would stick to that and would never change from it!

Dorothy had been gob-smacked!

What was all of this about? She had thought on the situation over and over again. He had not spoken to her in an amicable manner discussing any differences they may have had, but in an adamant, uncompromising and very dogmatic way. It was like he had just had a major wobbly, as Maria would say; Ian would probably have put it as him blowing a gasket. And all of this was provoked in him when hearing what Dorothy had spoken of from the simplicity of her heart and which, presumably he could not himself relate to! What had she said? What had she done? She gathered something had been triggered when talking about God's will and direction for her life. Whatever the cause in all of this was, it was true to say that Dorothy had been shaken and humiliated by the aggressive stance David had taken – and all of this to do with God?! Dorothy had been confronted with her first personal battle, and it did not come from someone outside of her circle of good friends but rather from a person within it!

The Bible reading gave her hope to trust in a power far greater than all others, a firm belief that God was always in control of the lives of those who loved Him even in the difficult times from which she was never ever going to be immune.

Dorothy got up and decided it was time to get ready for church. *Sometimes things can change suddenly,* she aspired to believe. *You do not know what a day shall bring forth!*

This aspiration of Dorothy's was a product of her personality and nature that was always determined to find hope in adversity and which she had proved in her early days when seeking help for herself from the book of Psalms. Now, the situation was quite different; it involved another person and not herself. What was making the situation sensitive to her was quite simple; the person in question happened to be a man she had grown to like! This made it all the more difficult and personal, for she had never walked down this pathway before.

———————————

In another bedroom a few miles away, a young lady was stirring in her bed. Unlike Dorothy's room, the heat had not kicked in and it was cold, or at least that's what Maria thought.

Her first reaction was to have a drink of tea and a request went from upstairs to downstairs as if from a tannoy in a factory or supermarket store asking for some member of staff, "Dad, can you make me a cup of tea please?"

No answer.

Maria knew she would have to go and get the cup of tea herself, for there was no way her dad could make it up the stairs; this she was well aware of, but normally there would be some response, and the kettle would go on.

Maria, dressing gown on, went downstairs to check on things. On some occasions her dad had fallen and struggled to get up again.

"Dad, where are you?"

Just as Maria was about to panic, who should come through the front door but Alfred, the very man, much to the relief of Maria.

"Oh! Dad, you had me worried! What have you been out for at this time?" Maria, noticing a bag in his hand, went on to say, "Don't tell me you've been to the shop! What on earth for? Did you run out of backa?"

"Questions, questions, questions!" responded Alfred. "I've been to the shop, yer right there. Here, Lass, let's make you a cuppa.

Are yeh feeling cold? There's been a bit of frost this mornin'; let's put some heat on for yeh."

It was quite clear Alfred was not going to let on what he had gone out to the shop for, but the most important thing as far as Maria was concerned was that he was safe.

<hr>

In yet another bedroom, a little girl was being dressed by her mummy. The heat was on, and it was nice and warm in that house, because Julia had the heat on low all night in her room! As is quite normal where young children are concerned, those clothes prepared by mum to dress one's child are not the ones the child wishes to wear. So it was with Julia.

"Please can I wear my new dress for church, Mummy?" Indeed, Julia had a mind of her own! That task done, it was breakfast time. Then, teeth were cleaned, and so the routine progressed nicely.

Mary phoned her brother to ask if he could come round a little earlier so that she could call at a shop on the way to church. There were a few things she needed to purchase to occupy her child with during the service; but with it being a little out of the way from the normal route, they would need extra time if they were not to be late. David responded by saying that it would not be a problem, but also added that he himself would not be coming with them to church. He would drop her and Julia off and pick them up afterwards.

As of late David had been going to his sister's church and not the one he normally went to – this was as a direct consequence of another person who also attended there – but not this morning; he had decided to stay away.

The time was approaching 9.45 a.m. and the occupants in the three houses were ready to leave for the morning service. This was to be taken by Pastor John Peterson with assistance from his wife, Miriam, who helped to care for the children when the singing and children's story had finished.

Dorothy would be leaving a little earlier together with John and Miriam; Mary and Julia were ready and waiting for their lift with David; Maria was also ready awaiting her lift from Ian.

Maria was in a quandary, having again lost sight of her dad; he was not in his chair! As she wandered through the kitchen and into the outside garden, she saw him sitting down on the concrete steps cleaning his boots.

"Going somewhere, Dad?" asked Maria humorously, for it was a rare sight that had met her eyes! Maria saw the shopping bag and a new shoe polish tin next to Alfred and gathered that he must have bought it when he went out early that morning.

What a joke! thought Maria smiling; he only has one pair of shoes, so he decides to clean them now!

The doorbell rang. Ian had arrived. Maria dashed straight to the door and let Ian come into the hallway, then she grabbed her coat off the stairs banister – and all this in the space of a few seconds.

Now, Alfred called out to Ian with a request, "Do yeh have room for one more, Lad?"

"Good morning, Mr Townsend! Why of course! Do you need a lift? Where would you like to be dropped off?"

Maria just stared at her dad suspiciously; she knew he was up to some mischief or other.

"That depends; where are you going to, Lad?"

"Why, to church of course. I've come to pick Maria up like I normally do, you know."

" Ah, that's good then; we both be going to the same place!"

"Dad, are you feelin' alright?" interrupted Maria. "Ian is just picking me up; we are going to church! It's Sunday!"

Maria reiterated Ian's words a second time, particularly emphasising the word church just in case he had not heard properly or had misunderstood. It did cross Maria's mind that her dad could have been drinking and that he was off his head, but no, this definitely was not the case as he would have smelled of it if he had and as it happened, Maria could not actually recollect him ever having touched any drink now for ages.

"I knows it's a Sunday! I ain't senile yet! Is there a law ses I can't come to church if I wants to?"

Alfred had finally gotten his message across, convincing everyone that he was serious in his desire to go to church with them. He was not drunk; he was fully compos mentis, and Maria found no apparent reason to question him any further but chose to simply accept his word, even though it was against all her reasoning and logic. In any case Alfred had taken himself to the car by now and was ready to go, so all three drove off to church together.

Maria, it had to be said, had mixed feelings as they were driving.

Will Dad be alright? she half-feared, wondering whether he would be an embarrassment or something. She did have to admit though that her dad looked very clean and tidy, and Ian was chatting away with him quite unperturbed. He had woken up early and been to the shop to buy polish to clean his boots; in short he had gone to a lot of trouble requiring some considerable effort on his part to say the least! Still, she was a mixture of suspense with excitement, bewilderment and a little apprehension. This was a new experience for her, as Alfred had never before been to Maria's church.

Unknown to Maria, Alfred had picked up the booklet she had left for him the previous evening, and he had read the Bible passages and verses written within it. As a consequence he was of a mind to meet up with Jesus, for he had read in Maria's book that Jesus invites people to come to him – and the best place to do that, he thought, was in a church!

Chapter 22

The Healing

All three vehicles converged towards the very same church, though Pastor John would say that the building in question was not the church at all, but those people who were believers were the church!

The vehicle carrying John, Miriam and Dorothy arrived first, as they needed to arrive before anyone else to open up, turn on the heating, and generally prepare the hall for the meeting. Their car was followed by Maria, Ian and Alfred's. They needed to prepare for the worship time with the rest of the band.

Alfred sat down in the middle of the front row by himself, watching with intrigue as his daughter rehearsed some of the songs singing into a microphone!

Many more people arrived straight afterwards including Mary and Julia. Dorothy chose to sit next to Alfred and not leave him by himself. On Dorothy's right sat Julia, who was determined not to sit at the back in spite of her mum's efforts to do so, but insisted upon sitting next to Dorothy at the front! Consequently, next to Julia was Mary, and next to Mary sat Miriam.

The meeting would normally last about one and a half hours. The programme was not rigid with a sequential set structure. Sometimes the pastor would preach near the beginning, other times right near the end; it usually depended upon how long the children's story took and whether or not there was to be a communion service. There would be prayer requests – mostly but not exclusively for the sick – and if the individuals were actually present themselves, they were always prayed for in person at the end of the meeting.

The eyes of Alfred were attentive to all that happened throughout the service, but he became particularly attentive when John preached God's Word.

Maria thought about her dad on more than one occasion.

How would he react? Why had he come to church at all that morning?

She peered towards her dad from time to time, actually nervous for him, and couldn't help wondering what he thought about it all.

Soon all would be revealed!

———————

Meanwhile, *Max's Coffee Bar* had received a customer for almost one hour now; he had been sitting at a table drinking an Americano with hot milk on the side and reading a newspaper. The gentleman's habit and preference was to always ask for hot milk, so that the coffee did not become cold as a result of adding too much milk.

Why on earth, he thought to himself, *are Sunday newspapers so thick with relatively little of interest!*

Well, that was David Osborne's grumpy opinion as he placed the newspaper down and then glanced at his watch to keep a special eye on the time.

David's state of mind was confused; he was cross with himself and generally fed up with the turn of events recently. Why he had reacted so with Dorothy who, he had to admit, was speaking sincerely to him about those things that were close to her heart, was beneath him; he was ashamed now looking back. He thought to himself just how arrogant and rude he had been!

Nevertheless, the fact remained that David was repulsed by her words, simple and sincere as they were. They touched within him a delicate and sensitive area, which he had not realised existed until then, and his pride had fought against her simplicity. Her childlike faith had spoken to him deeply as if uprooting within him his own hypocrisy. She was authentic; he wasn't. She was sincere in what she believed; he was not!

David compared himself with Dorothy. What exactly did she have that was missing from his life? Certainly, there was something! He had all the years of religion from childhood; she had all the personal knowledge about God. He had all the good works that he considered made him a good and outstanding Christian; she had relatively little to speak of, and according to Dorothy she had only been a Christian a mere four months!

Had she not been baptised as a baby? thought David. *Just like me?*

This particular matter had proved to be somewhat interesting when they were both sitting together at the Indian restaurant alone. Their conversation together had gone something like this:

'Were you baptised as a baby, Dorothy?'

'Yes, I believe I was, David.'

'Well, are we not both Christians then, of a sort?

"David, I'm not so sure that I was a Christian before. I mean... yes, I believed in God, but so do many others who never go to church... and also the devil does too, so what makes us a Christian?"

"Well, you do those things the church teaches, and you should be alright. How do you see it, Dorothy?"

"David, I have basically started a new life of faith – faith in a personal God and in the Bible, which I believe is the Word of God. I started reading the Psalms several months ago when I just craved God's help in my life. I went to church from time to time, but I did not get anything from it. I liked what I read and was encouraged to believe. That's how it all started for me."

"Well, I do not care for all this talk about Jesus, Jesus! I mean... it sounds over the top to me,

Dorothy, and I don't wish to offend you in saying that. Odd people go off like that!"

"David, you are not being kind when you say that and even worse if you actually believe it!"

"Well, that is the way I see it, Dorothy. Just imagine what my mates at work would think if I were to talk like that; they would probably think I had gone mad! They are mostly decent guys. I would say they are alright and are not what you would call sinners, after all God loves us all, so what is the big deal? I cannot believe these friends of mine are all going to hell!"

"I am very surprised to hear you talk like this, David. There is nothing more to say. I certainly do not wish to argue with you. I am fully aware of your opinion ... Please take me home..."

David was still in *Max's*, and as these recollections of the conversation with Dorothy went through his mind, he felt that irreparable damage had been done.

What bothered him, however, was Dorothy's character and integrity. He could not gainsay her views; all he could do was mock and criticise and that in a most defensive and arrogant manner!

David felt guilty. Somehow, he just knew she was more likely to be correct in her thinking than he was! She was not odd or mad, as he had tended to imply regarding people who held similar views to her, but she did seem to him to be outside of the box and the status quo. Even so, he knew this was not a real argument of any significance whatsoever, for most young people today were different to the rest in some way or another, and no one really cared about that. It certainly did not imply that because they were different, they had to be wrong. David was in a quandary. He had seemingly nothing to base his arguments upon regarding his religious upbringing and beliefs. He did not particularly know what the Bible said, for he never read it. Now, he was confronted with a person in Dorothy who was quite different to himself and actually read the Bible; it was more a part of her life than his. Was this her crime?

Though David would never admit it, if the thoughts and intents of his heart were put under the microscope of scrutiny, they would reveal deep prejudices, some of which were:

You are not to be too different to everyone else and certainly not to the old school of thought, which could never ever be wrong. Too many people believe like this! They cannot all be wrong!

Surely, those churches with the finest buildings and pomp and splendour must be the most important! If your church was in a simple building or even a hired hall, then it could never be mainstream or that important!

Now, David was a thoughtful person with some measure of integrity, in spite of all of these differences and misgivings that had become manifest under the spotlight of Dorothy; she was to blame for this! Her light shone and illuminated thoughts, views and prejudices that he had never thought he had.

David felt guilty alright, and that was putting it mildly. He knew that Ian and Maria and many others would not be on his side if they were to be told what he had said to Dorothy; she was far too well loved and respected!

Could David do anything to rectify the situation? Would he be willing to change from his religious facade and face the challenges of the real deal like Dorothy? As David thought of her purity, her honesty, in fact everything about her, he felt ashamed and wished now he could be like her in place of all his wretchedness!

David observed the time; it was 11:45, and the service was due to end about midday. He needed to be driving to the church to collect his sister.

When David arrived at the church, the car park was full, so he parked his car on a side street. Meanwhile, inside the building, various people from the congregation were walking to the front to ask for prayer. At this time it was normal for some of the congregation to leave, especially those with children. The meeting had essentially finished.

Alfred stood up to be among those who came forward, and as Pastor John came to him, he discreetly asked Alfred what he desired prayer for. What reached his ears came as a bit of a surprise.

"Pastor, I've come to meet with Jesus. Can yeh help me?"

John beckoned his wife to come and join him, and taking Alfred aside, the three sat down together leaving others to pray for those who remained. John talked quite softly to Alfred, asking him about himself and exactly what he would like John to do.

"Well, I ain't been no church goer, yeh know… not since my mar took me as a lad, and well… it was like this, about nine years ago…"

Alfred began to recite how he had been a farmhand for thirty-seven years, that he had had an accident with a tractor giving him an injured leg and forcing him to retire, how he had blamed the Almighty for years regarding his state, and further, how he had taken to drink and that his wife had moved out to her sisters.

"I just got my Maria now; over there she is, bless her. She's an angel to me."

John looked at Maria and called her, "Maria, why did you not tell me that your father was here? This is just great! Alfred, I am very pleased to meet you. So what would you like me to do for you, Alfred? Would you like me to pray for you and your situation?"

"Pastor, I been readin' some things out of the Bible yeh know, and I wants to say sorry to God for what I been."

"Well, that is wonderful, Alfred!"

John talked to Alfred about what it meant to come to God through Jesus and how He had died for each one of us on the cross so that we might be forgiven.

"Yeah, I gathered that much; I was readin' all about that. Well, that's why I'm here, see? I did feel bad inside when I saw He did that for me – and I been cursing Him all these years!

"Yer Worship, I'm an unworthy sinner. I knows I am, but I would still likes to thank Him and ask Him if He'd forgive me! I would give Him my life, what's left of it, if He would; I would serve Him for as long as I live!"

John was moved with great compassion upon hearing all of these responses from the simple heart of a simple man!

They continued to read together, discussing as they went, and Alfred became quite tearful, so that Maria came to his side and Dorothy stood nearby.

"Yer see," said Alfred, "Jesus said in one of them verses that the one who comes to Him He will by no means cast out – that were it."

Alfred was quite pleased with himself that he was able to quote the verse almost exactly as he had read it from the booklet given him by Maria. "That's what He said. Well, I reckoned that were an invitation, is that right? 'Cos I couldn't have dared come otherwise!"

"Alfred, that is exactly right," replied John. He was amazed; never before had he seen such simple faith!

Now what John, Miriam, Maria and Dorothy witnessed next they would never forget for the rest of their lives. It would be an image recalled from time to time, speaking to them of this very event taking place at this very moment in time!

"Will God really forgive me for what I been?" cried Alfred, and no sooner had he uttered those very words than tears poured down from his eyes like two dripping taps, and he sat down again with both hands over his face.

John knew this was the moment to do what God had called him to do as a minister of the Gospel – to lead this man to Him!

Alfred's faith and trust in receiving God's Word for himself was evident. He had acknowledged his unworthiness in a repentant manner; he had believed and responded to God's invitation to come to Him; he understood that when Jesus died upon the cross, it was for him personally! Yes, his understanding was small, but what he did know had been clearly revealed to him by God and that was very evident.

During the next few seconds, just prior to praying for Alfred, John gave thought to what he was about to do, and as a consequence there came certain truths from the Bible that went through his mind and confirmed to him loud and clear just in case he had any doubts within himself regarding what was taking place before him.

.... I did not come to call the righteous but sinners to repentance.

Alfred satisfied that!

.... if you have faith as a mustard seed....

You do not need a lot of faith, so Alfred qualified again!

....not many wise according to the flesh, not many mighty, not many noble are called....

Alfred most certainly qualified!

John laid his hands upon Alfred and began to pray for him. This action was, as a whole, accepted as a normal physical procedure, though in today's society it was not always wise to do so without asking the person concerned what they would prefer.

As soon as John had laid his hands upon Alfred's head and shoulder, there came a great presence of the Holy Spirit upon all that stood nearby! It could be described in essence just like a fireball that hit Alfred primarily, but its heat was felt by all who were close to him!

John found he had received a great sense of liberty, faith and assurance as he prayed! His words were not being read from a book! They just came out as he felt inspired and prompted to speak – just like water flowing from a gushing fountain – and that straight from his heart.

Pastor John's praying seemed to draw in the prayers of those who were standing around. Everyone was now praying; hands were raised up; tears were falling!

Suddenly the praying ceased. Alfred got up and with a gleeful smile said, "Wow! What were that?"

Then, as he was thanking everyone, something unusual and out of the ordinary happened!

What took place in the ensuing moments was to be a controversial talking point for weeks to come!

All around the church hall people were gazing at the noisy scene at the front; they witnessed a man jumping around and shouting at the top of his voice, "My leg, my leg is on fire! Wow! Wow!"

Maria stepped forward to support her dad for he had forgotten to use his stick whilst getting up from his seat.

Alfred's countenance exhibited great amazement, surprise and joy for he was walking using both legs unaided!

"The Almighty has touched me leg! It's burning with fire I tell thee!"

Alfred would not stop; he leaped up and down! It was an amazing sight – to some, not so to others!

Etiquette and propriety seemed to vanish as Alfred slowly went up the long aisle towards the main door, shouting out with joy and leaping about on his two feet!

Some of those who were left in the building looked on with astonishment; others appeared quite embarrassed with what met their eyes. Some exhibited great joy and also shouted out with praise and thanks, but some doubted and turned away; they were not happy at all!

Some young people were very happy with the spectacle and were seen scuttling around with their mobile cameras taking pictures and enjoying every moment. Their generation had never witnessed such a thing before – only read about it in the Bible!

"Awesome! This is really cool! The old man's been healed! Let's go closer!"

"Take a video, take a video! This is fantastic!"

These were typical comments heard around the church wherever there were young people gathered.

Standing at the back stood a tall, young gentleman observing these happenings in a sober fashion. He had ventured in to see what was delaying his sister, Mary, for people had been leaving for some time, but there had been no sign of her and Julia. The scene that met his eyes was such as he had never witnessed before – not in any church, not even in this particular church.

Ian saw the man standing at the back of the church and recognised him has David Osborne. Running over to him, he spoke with great excitement and glee, "Hey! What about that then? Awesome! Awesome! Alfred's got saved, and the Lord has healed him as well!"

David was momentarily stuck to the spot in wonder and amazement! He heard some people speaking in a strange language at the front of the church, which seemed to bring upon him an awe of fear and reverence for it brought with it a consciousness of the presence of God!

David pondered everything before his eyes and ears thinking, *Surely God is in this place!*

He felt within him a strong compulsion to go forward towards the front of the church, whilst Alfred at the same time was steadily making his way towards the back so that they met at a point somewhere in the middle.

Alfred had never seen David before, yet he spoke to him with great boldness and confidence as though he did know him.

"Hey, young man, don't tell me there is no God! He's real alright! Look what he's done for me!" Alfred indicated by pointing to his leg.

"That is fantastic for you!" replied David in a respectful fashion, for he dare not say otherwise; he was determined to question nothing.

"He's true to His Word; that I do know!" continued Alfred.

Maria was following closely behind her father; Dorothy followed Maria, and others came, all watching the spectacle before them. Pastor John and Miriam stood at the same point where they had prayed for Alfred gazing at the scene with utter amazement, hardly believing their eyes.

Soon they were all clustered together, congregating around Alfred. David looked at Dorothy; Dorothy looked at David! Dorothy's eyes shone with warmth and kindness inviting reconciliation; David's eyes revealed a heavy load with some remorse, so that after gazing into her eyes for a few seconds, he could not help but look downwards at the floor as if in shame.

Whilst everyone else buzzed with excitement and conversation, David continued walking forward. As he passed Dorothy, he acknowledged her with a half-smile and whispered the words, "I'm so very sorry, Dorothy; please forgive me."

None seemed to notice David as he continued to walk towards the front as if to meet with his Maker, but Dorothy did, and turning aside she followed, walking just a few yards behind him. David stood still momentarily; he looked as though he wished to speak with Pastor John, who was busy talking with his wife. When Miriam noticed him, she beckoned her husband to give David some attention.

Dorothy stopped and stood back, for John and David had sat down and where talking together. Before long John and David could be seen praying together! Dorothy, observing everything, was quite moved within herself. She turned to one side moving further away, not wishing to distract or in any way intrude upon the situation if per chance David turned slightly and saw her standing there.

Meanwhile, Alfred was still talking with a whole group of people; suddenly he was the man of the moment!

Who is he? thought some.

I know this man, said others, talking among themselves. *I have seen him in town on occasions, but he could hardly walk then! Look at him now!*

Alfred, by now, just wanted to go home. He needed to get his head around things. All of the excitement was making him tired! Ian and Maria led him through the crowd to oblige him, and whilst making their way to the car a gentleman carrying a large shoulder bag took photographs of Alfred with a large professional looking camera.

They drove off taking Alfred back to his room and to his chair, which for once had gone cold through the absence of its occupant. One item had been left behind in the church however; it was Alfred's old crutch! This would most likely be placed amongst the rest of the umbrellas, clothes and other forgotten items in a dusty cupboard.

It was very quiet now; the humdrum and melodrama had finished. Dorothy had sat down towards the back of the church along with Mary and Julia. They were all waiting now for David, who had been sitting with John for about half an hour.

Mary had conversed with Dorothy regarding her brother, mentioning how he had come home the previous evening quite perturbed and seemingly upset. He had not told his sister everything, and it needed Dorothy to explain a little more so that Mary saw the whole picture. The time spent waiting for David had provided an opportune moment to do this.

Eventually David and John stood up together and went over to the party patiently waiting for them.

If David and Dorothy had much to say to one another, this was not the opportune time to do so, for Mary and little Julia needed to be going home. Julia was hungry and tired, which was never a good combination! Instead, they looked warmly at one another in passing and discreetly arranged to meet up the following evening for a meal in order to talk. David had whispered the words, "I must see you, if you will. Can I pick you up at 7:30 tomorrow? I would like to take you out for a meal."

Dorothy had replied in the affirmative.

Meanwhile, John had joined Miriam and begun clearing away. Life had to go on. The mundane jobs were waiting for them and the rest of the team.

"Everything is rather flat now following on from all of that," commented John. "Who would have thought it? A stranger comes in to church; he turns out to be Maria's father, gets saved, and then gets healed in a most remarkable manner! Why, he was jumping and shouting like the lame man outside the temple gate called Beautiful! I have never witnessed anything like it before, Dear."

"It was just wonderful! Wonderful is the word!" replied Miriam. "Come, let's finish off and take Dorothy home. I'm dying for a cup of tea; I don't know about you."

"What's for dinner, Love?"

"You will see," replied Miriam.

Chapter 23

David Seeks Advice from His Sister

"What made you go out to the front this morning?"

The question was posed to David by his sister as they drove home after church. They both thought it incredible what had happened that morning regarding Alfred, and it was discussed at great length; however, Mary was more curious regarding her brother's well-being of late, especially regarding a certain person with whom conversation had not been all that amicable recently.

"I had not been feeling right in myself. I really blew it with all the things I said to Dorothy; I just lost it. Ever since then, I've had no peace and have been feeling very guilty! After all of the good things I have said about her in the past too – just how much I really liked her and everything. I felt a great necessity to at least get myself right; that's why I went forward this morning. I wanted for myself what she has. I must say though, upon entering the church I had this overwhelming sense of what I can only describe as God's presence! It was just as if God was there in person; it was that real! I can tell you, Mary; I became desperate to get right with God!"

"That is something quite special, David. I must admit, though; I was sorry to hear what had happened between you and Dorothy! Do you still like her?"

"What do you think? Of course I do, but I am still wondering whether I have inflicted irreparable damage. What can Dorothy possibly think of me now after saying what really must have been offensive things – and personal to her? How stupid and pig-headed I was! The thought of actually hurting Dorothy even now causes me pain! How I wish I could change things!"

"Don't you worry, David; if Dorothy is worth her salt – and I know very well she is – she will accept your apology, but you will have to make it up to her. You have been repentant today with God; now you need to humble yourself and do the same with her, if as you say you really love her."

"But I didn't say I loved her!"

"True! Fine! Well, do you love her, David?"

"'Course I do!"

Mary laughed, "That is so typical; men easily say the wrong things and afterwards regret it, but never seemingly say the right!

"Anyway, David, I'm very proud of you for what you did this morning. It was the right thing. I know it sounds like... well, I told you so… but as I have said to you many times before, going to church does not make you a Christian!

"Dorothy is like me; we both came to the Lord in a personal way, knowing we needed him in our lives. We both came to Jesus just as we were and received Him for ourselves, like it says in the Bible… What is the verse I am thinking of? Ha! Yes, '…but as many as received Him, to them He gave the right to become children of God to those who believe in His name!'

"It has to be personal, just like you did today. David, believe you me, your life will never be the same from now on if you really meant it!"

Mary leaned over to kiss her brother on the cheek. She had made him feel good upon hearing her counsel and encouragement.

Soon they arrived home, and once Julia was settled and down for a nap, the two could sit together again. It couldn't have come soon enough for David; he was eager to continue talking about his new life and of course hear what Mary had to say about his chances with Dorothy.

"Mary, you will have to show me where all those Scriptures are. Will you help me? To be honest, I don't have a clue."

"All in good time, David, but you have done the most important thing you possibly could, you know? It's not based upon how much you know or what you have done, good or bad; it's all to do with your heart! This is more important to God than anything else, believe you me. The amazing thing, David, is that God saves you entirely by His Grace through faith in Jesus Christ! That's how it is!

"This morning, how did you feel? I take it you prayed with the pastor and made a decision, yes?"

"Yes, I did. It was like a very peaceful moment, Mary, like I was close to God; it felt as if a great load was lifted from me, and I was suddenly right with God! It seems funny to say that after what I have done, and yet that's how I actually felt. Can you believe that, Mary? Does that seem stupid and arrogant to you?"

"No, not at all; that's what grace is. I do like the way you describe it, David. That's awesome!"

"Mind you, Mary; I felt a bit stupid when I got outside, as if it was all a load of rubbish. I am being honest with you."

"That's what happens when a sinner enters the Kingdom of God. The devil doesn't like it! I'll share with you the parable of the sower if you like. Once you are born again, you find this is what happens, so we have to start living by faith and not by our feelings anymore. It's what God says in His Word that counts. Whenever you read it and affirm that you believe it, the devil runs away. Don't you worry, David; the Power that's on your side is greater than that which is not! Just put your trust in God from now on. You will still have problems like anyone else, so always turn to God and trust in His Word."

"Mary, you sound so knowledgeable! I've never heard you talk quite like this before."

"That's because in the past, whenever I may have spoken God's Word, it never actually made sense to you, but now you can hear it and understand it because you are receiving it for yourself. God does a work in our hearts, David, the moment we receive and accept Him; that's why you understand me now talking to you about the Bible and things. It's all because God has given you a new heart to believe and receive. Believe you me, there is no upper limit on what you are going to see and understand. I am so proud of you, my brother!"

"I'm pleased you are my sister, Mary."

"Now, that is a big change coming from you, David! Please keep it up. I'm glad you are my brother too."

Pastor John, Miriam and Dorothy arrived home about twenty minutes later than David and Mary. The conversation whilst travelling home had been full of Alfred's conversion and healing, as well as David's coming to Christ!

"He was walking without his crutch; that speaks for itself," said John.

"Yes, Dear, we know that, but I believe there were some of our congregation who seemed quite sceptical about it all. I have a strong feeling things will never be the same ever again."

"What on earth do you mean, Miriam?"

John only tended to call his wife by her name when trying to get her attention or when he was somewhat serious with her. John was serious.

"Well," continued Miriam, "things may change for the better in some quarters, namely with all the young people without exception and probably all those who are born again believers; but elsewhere, things could become worse."

"Yes, I think I know what you mean, Dear. Alfred's experience will draw a line through the congregation between those who rejoice in the miraculous and welcome the presence of the Lord and those... who don't! Is that what you mean?"

"Yes! In a nutshell, that's right. How do you feel about that, John?"

The criteria that applied to John when speaking to his wife by her first name did not apply in reverse; Miriam equally used the names Dear, my Dear and John when referring to her husband. However, if she ever spoke to John saying 'husband' and nothing else, then what followed could be serious!

"What will be will be!" replied John with an air of resignation that yielded to his conviction that one must put what God is doing for His own glory above all that suits people.

"I always try to speak God's Word just as it is written. That is my job, my commission, just like the disciples of old who said, 'Is it better to please man or to please God?' "

"And would you worry if numbers dropped in the church as a result, my Dear?"

"Now you are being pessimistic! If anything, numbers will increase; I guarantee it. Why, Maria and Ian and the rest of them will bring all their friends into church after this, and what about Alfred? He will attract some, I believe – but even if this was not the case and numbers should decrease, it is God's church not ours! He is in charge and will show us what to do!"

"That's faith and trust, hey Dorothy?" asserted Miriam. She agreed with everything John had said and so also did Dorothy, who had been rather quiet until now; however, this frank talk from the pastor assured her as to his genuineness in the faith in a manner that she had never heard before. Dorothy later described his honest deliberations as a refreshing exposition of faith and the putting of God's Word first come what may.

Dorothy added another important matter just to remind everyone that David had seemingly come to the Lord as well that morning!

"Yes, indeed!" John exclaimed, for he had temporally forgotten. "I wonder what brought that about; do you know anything, Dorothy?!"

Chapter 24

Dorothy and Miriam Discuss Relationships

That evening, because of the time of the year, darkness drew in early. It was getting cold and frosty outside, and John turned up the heat. Being rather large, the lounge where John and Dorothy sat soon got cold enough to be uncomfortable if the heat was not increased. John never liked the temperature lower than twenty degrees if he was sitting for an appreciable period of time, and Dorothy was not going to argue about that.

It had been a lazy, sleepy afternoon, and Miriam's roast lamb dinner contributed to that significantly, especially because it was followed by a deep apple and blackberry crumble with custard – Dorothy's favourite!

Miriam had decided to make some cakes in the kitchen for the following day when a group of young mum's where coming round for their fortnightly meet and chat, so John had sat down with Dorothy having a light conversation and a cup of old English tea.

"It was very good to see David Osborne out at the front this morning, and he didn't come into the meeting until right near the end. A very pleasant chap he is, Dorothy! Sincere and quite remorseful he was; it is always a good sign. Why, you know him; don't you, Dorothy? My goodness, of course you do! He helped you with the removal, and Miriam said he took you all out for a meal afterwards. That was very kind of him, and afterwards… Oh! I do beg your pardon, Dorothy, but I recollect now that your conversation was not too… was not very agreeable. I'm sorry, but my words ran away with me just then. How are things now, if I may ask?"

Dorothy looked at John to decide just how to reply, for it was clearly second-hand information he had received from Miriam; and John, it would seem, had most likely taken in only the gist of it – in other words, very little!

Dorothy decided to emphasise a more positive approach to the situation rather than regurgitate those words she had had with David in the Indian restaurant, and so proceeded to talk of events that happened in church.

"Yes, we had certain words together previously, but judging from this morning, things may have taken a turn. He was actually apologetic to me. Well, we shall see! Mary said he wasn't supposed to be coming to church, but he did. I wonder why?"

"Well, a jolly good thing he did, Dorothy!"

Miriam decided to check up on her husband, having heard his talking from in the kitchen. "John! I do hope you are behaving yourself. I can hear you from in here. What has he been saying to you, Dorothy?" Miriam had finished her cakes now and had come to join Dorothy and John in the lounge.

"He is fine, Miriam, honestly!" smiled Dorothy.

John decided to get up then and leave the two ladies together for a while, and in the process took a cake from the plate that Miriam had placed upon the table. He was getting the message that this would be a far better arrangement if he left them alone.

"Dorothy, would you like to try one of my cakes? Clearly John did! They are cool enough to eat now."

"I think I can manage just one, thank you. Can I have this iced one with the cherry on top?"

"Of course, you help yourself to one... Dorothy, I expect John has already talked about this judging by what I heard earlier, but don't you think it was wonderful what happened this morning, about David I mean? And after all that you told me he had said to you before!"

"Yes! I am as surprised as you are. It was quite amazing really. Who could have known it?"

"Well, God did; that's for sure," replied Miriam.

Now, the two ladies were on the same wavelength and free to speak about anything; they could talk and talk unhindered for as long as they wished.

Having started with David as the initial topic, they went on to discuss friends, boy- friends, relationships and more; marriage, sex before marriage, co-habiting couples or partners as they are called; in fact, anything that tickled their fancy was on the agenda! It was good for both of them to talk. It developed mutual trust and understanding between one another.

Finally, it got down to the nitty gritty.

"Miriam, if there are problems near the beginning of a possible relationship with someone, does that suggest that things are not meant to be with that relationship?"

This was a very thoughtful question from Dorothy, and it did not take rocket science for Miriam to figure out where it was coming from either. There was no simple answer. Miriam would attempt to summarise many points of view in her reply to Dorothy; it was important for her, seeing as she had asked the question in earnest, to see different scenarios and then make her own decision. It had to be her choice.

"First and foremost we commit our prospective relationships to the Lord but ultimately the choice is your responsibility," replied Miriam. "I would say that problems can occur at any time in a relationship, Dorothy, in the beginning or otherwise. That does not necessarily mean that you are not meant to be together, for if it did then John and I would have been in and out of our relationship dozens of times – and being a Christian does not make us immune from problems either. John would say, 'When it rains, it rains on everyone equally!'

"We do all make mistakes and always will; none of us is perfect, and with God's help we are learning how to live our lives every day in His way. It is not easy, because we as individuals are all different to one another.

"The best thing for both of you, at the beginning, is to individually and independently seek to follow and obey God in your own personal life and agree together to share with each other everything. It is important to be open and free with one another. An important ingredient in a healthy relationship, which will move on to marriage, is to learn how to forgive one another. Someone once said, 'It is only by making mistakes and hurting one another that we learn one of the greatest of human joys – forgiveness!'

"And here is another saying, 'Love isn't finding a perfect person. It's seeing an imperfect person perfectly!' There is some truth in both of these quotes.

"Clearly it is good to have a friendship at first that might then lead on to a steady relationship over some period of time without, I would say, intimacy for the reasons we talked about earlier. If you can do this, in my opinion it will be better for you, but not everything is cut and dried; that's why we need to pray and seek

God's wisdom and clear guidance. In my opinion it is always wiser to seek a relationship with God first. He actually knows all things and wants the best for us. He knows what will really make us happy; sometimes we think we know, but we don't really. My mother used to say, 'Don't rush; don't push!' Time proves all things. In this way, you can pray and ask God with confidence that he will guide you regarding a relationship with someone. I believe He will show you if you really wish to know one way or another!

"We know all that glitters is not gold, and you don't judge a book by its cover. Dorothy! The bottom line is, if you really love someone, you will know. God makes it simple somehow when He knows you love Him; He just does!"

Now upon this very same evening a young man, who had recently given his heart to the Lord, had been having great discourse with his sister regarding his decision, she being fairly knowledgeable in these things herself.

Mary Osborne was completely and utterly full of unspeakable joy whilst talking with her brother, David. Never before had she been able to converse and share with him regarding such things, but now everything had changed! David drank everything in like water. He asserted that it was good to be right with God!

Now by a strange coincidence – if, that is, there are such things as coincidences for nothing happens outside of the providence of Almighty God – David wished to confer with his sister about a certain matter that was upon his heart, and remarkably the subject had just been spoken of by two other people elsewhere in another room in another house! He changed the subject of his discourse with Mary to the more nitty gritty details regarding relationships and began by posing the very same question that Dorothy had asked of Miriam or at least with words to that effect.

"Mary, if two people were to begin a relationship together but had difficulties near the beginning, would that…"

Now, it did not take rocket science for Mary to perceive just where this was coming from, and so she proceeded in a gentle but realistic manner with David; and whether by coincidence or not, she expounded to him very similar views to those of another certain lady who had spoken with Dorothy that very same evening.

And so it happened that the two persons, whether by coincidence or not, received similar counsel that day.

Chapter 25

Dorothy and David Meet

Of all places, David and Dorothy had arranged to meet in the Indian restaurant! Of course, their last visit to this place had ended on a sour note, and it may not therefore have been considered the most appropriate time to go back to the same restaurant; yet, there was a reason.

David was quite thoughtful. He knew that Dorothy quite liked an Indian meal occasionally, and this particular restaurant was her favourite and probably the best place in town. Why should she have to forfeit ever going back there again because of a bad memory? Consequently, David thought it a good idea to go back straight away to the very same place so as to leave a good memory in her mind and not a bad one, if that is the outcome this time was to be a much better experience than the first; he firmly believed it would be.

David was a changed man. He had humbled himself; he felt as free as a bird! Now, all he wanted was Dorothy! His heart ached at every thought of her. It was like he had thrown a brick of gold into a dustbin. Was it too late to retrieve it?

Dorothy was very pleased with his change spiritually but remained nervous. Meeting with a man on her own was in itself an ominous task normally, but of late she had made good progress in that area. No, Dorothy was a little nervous because there was no telling just how things would go! It was the unexpected, the unknown factor, that caused her apprehension. She was afraid of doing the wrong thing.

Did Dorothy find David good looking? Having had that conversation with him, the answer to that question had become completely irrelevant! David was indeed a very likeable and handsome man; this she knew from the beginning when she first met him, but time had showed a different side to him, one that would never be acceptable to her in spite of all of his other qualifications. Dorothy was feeling cautious but tried to be hopeful nevertheless. Things could only get better, she reassured herself, now that he had come to the Lord. Let Him be her guide!

Dorothy looked in her wardrobe for something appropriate to wear. A dress would be the order of the day, she thought. Though this was not always considered the most popular choice amongst ladies, preference seemingly being directed to more body-tight clothing declaring the precise shape of one's figure from top to bottom, she was well aware of what David thought on their first visit to the restaurant; he had hardly taken his eyes off her!

I think I will wear a similar dress again, thought Dorothy. *Men do love to see a lady in a dress it seems, no matter what the dictates of fashion may be. They are conservative at heart, loving a woman, as they would say, to be a woman – in short, wearing a dress!*

David was getting himself ready too. He had heard Mary's words ringing in his ears all that day, '…if Dorothy is worth her salt – and I know very well she is – she will accept your apology, but you will have to make it up to her. You have been repentant today with God; now you need to humble yourself and do the same with her, if as you say you really love her…'

Some of her words had really stuck out to him as being very important, namely to make it up to her and for him to humble himself.

David decided to check his motives right to the very heart of his being, and he asked himself various questions to test his inner self.

Is she worth it? Yes.

Would you really humble yourself? Yes.

… even if all of your mates were there watching what you did? Yes.

…even when she goes on about God's will? Yes, in fact that would be awesome. I need to learn from Dorothy about these things.

"David, are you feeling alright? I can hear you talking to yourself!" Mary had just gone upstairs and walked passed the bedroom where David was changing.

"How do I look, Sis?" said David, opening the bedroom door and completely ignoring her question.

Mary looked at her brother, stood back a step to view the whole man, then commented, "David, you look very smart, very smart indeed! That suit is so sharp, not a crease. Well done! I'm sure she will be impressed. Is that a new suit, David?"

"Now, why do you ask such a thing?" replied David in a smug manner as if to say 'of course it is!'

It had become fairly dark outside. The worst of rush hour traffic was about over, and David glanced out of the lounge window as if looking for something or someone. And then it happened! A black taxi arrived outside Mary's house. David rushed to the door shouting goodbye to Mary as he left.

David could have easily driven there himself, but he had insisted on picking Dorothy up in a different manner – and what better way than in a taxi, but this was going to be no ordinary taxi! He had particularly asked the cab company for a new taxi, and if this was not normal practice, then he would see him right with the price. He got a new one! He further explained to the driver that this was a very special occasion and would he kindly take the role of a chauffeur by opening the door for the lady on arrival at the restaurant. The gentleman smiled and reassured him that he would do just that.

The taxi stopped at Dorothy's home with the Petersons. The driver, after putting on his smart cap and jacket, went out himself and rang the doorbell.

Dorothy was taken by surprise to see the smart looking cab driver meeting her at the door asking for her, "Taxi for Miss McGuire!"

"A taxi is here!" shouted Dorothy to Miriam excitedly.

"A taxi, did you say?" said Miriam surprised.

"Yes, David has sent me a taxi… and oh! He is inside waiting for me!"

"Then you had better get going, Miss McGuire!" said John humorously, having overheard the conversation and having reached the door just in time to see her go.

Dorothy looked beautiful! She wore a brown leather coat over her dress, and she had also gone to great lengths with her appearance. Her long, chestnut hair waved perfectly onto her shoulders and around her chin; her contagious smile and star-like eyes were stunning!

This gentleman is a very lucky man indeed, thought the cab driver as he opened the rear door for Dorothy, where David sat waiting for her.

"Dorothy, you look very beautiful," was David's fitting greeting to Dorothy as she sat next to him. "We are going to that Indian restaurant. I hope that is alright with you? "

Dorothy was experiencing a high level of emotion at that particular moment, the occasion making her feel a little heady, so that she hardly heard what David had just said to her. She simply replied, "Of course; that is good. Thank you, David."

Upon reaching the restaurant, the chauffeur did what was required of him; he walked around the car and opened the door for the lady.

"Have a good evening, My Lady, and you too, Sir! Just give me a buzz ten minutes before you wish to leave, Sir, and I will come and pick you up; thank you, Sir."

Now the cab driver was a polite gentleman who fit the occasion perfectly. Nevertheless, his final thank you to David was not without purpose, for David could be seen discreetly placing something in his hand as he left.

Now, David and Dorothy were together at last!

It was not expedient to pry upon their evening together or their conversation; it was too special, too personal too intimate – and after all, everyone deserves to have some privacy at some time, and this was their time!

Certain things, however, just had to be spoken of! During the course of their meal, a bunch of red roses was delivered to Dorothy. Her complexion went a similar colour to that of the flowers briefly, just for a moment, then she leaned over to kiss David upon his cheek to say thank you.

Now, curries being what they are, they could easily leave traces of tasty sauce upon the lips of those who ate them. In David's case, it was straight forward; he could ask for a hot moist towel smelling with an aroma of lemon and use it to wipe his mouth.

Dorothy's situation was not so convenient; she was wearing a little something or other upon her lips, and a towel was not really appropriate.

"Whoops!" said Dorothy, laughing and smiling in sequence; I shall have to pass on that."

As they both stood up to leave, David walked over to Dorothy and gave her an envelope. Upon opening it, she found a beautiful card with words written inside which said:

The fountains mingle with the river,
And the rivers with the ocean;
The winds of heaven mix forever,
With a sweet emotion;
Nothing in the world is single;
All things by a law divine
In one another's being mingle;-
Why not I with thine?

See! The mountains kiss high
            Heaven,
And the waves clasp one another;
No sister flower would be forgiven,
    If it disdained it's brother;
And the sunlight clasps the earth,
And the moonbeams kiss the
            sea;-
What are all these kissings worth,
    If though kiss not me?

P.B. Shelley
(1792-1822)

Upon reading its contents, Dorothy's heart trembled; she knew the inevitable was going to happen! David held her hands in his, then drawing her closer to him said, "Thank you for this wonderful evening, Dorothy; I do love you very much!"

Dorothy gazed into David's eyes. She saw him at last for who he was – the person! Realising just how much David meant to her, she uttered similar words to David.

"Thank you as well, David, for a most wonderful time that I will never forget. I love you too, David!"

David moved closer to Dorothy if that were possible and gently kissed her upon the lips; she did not object but simply smiled at him and kissed him back in similar fashion.

Now, David had tasted just a little hint of curry with his kiss! It did not matter at all; David loved Dorothy, and he loved curry!

As it happened, Dorothy had tasted a little hint of lemon with her kiss! That did not matter either; Dorothy loved David, and she loved lemon!

A Note from the Author

When greeted with the usual *'Good morning and how are you?'* one rarely receives a genuine heartfelt response if you declare the bad news, *'I'm not feeling good!'* (... except, perhaps from a lady!)

Rather, what is more than likely to develop in such cases is an inhibited quietness followed by a sense of awkwardness filling the air!

This traditional greeting is not particularly convenient in some situations as we all know, but that is our custom nevertheless and we live with it! Imagine though the effect upon someone suffering from a particularly bad moment of depression! The individual will surely feel pressurised into not telling the truth in most cases or at least not revealing the whole truth. What follows is reclusive isolation!

As described in this story, one of the greatest difficulties is the stigma associated with all mental illnesses, and some responses even from close friends and family can be:

It's not physical therefore not real! Get over it! Pull yourself together. Medication? You don't want to go down that road do you?

It has been my desire, having known the traumas of depression myself, to highlight this condition and attempt to vividly describe what it can be like. In so doing I have proceeded to show how faith in God can considerably help, especially if part of a package consisting of support, good advice and suitable medication if necessary – this was the prescription in Miriam's letter to Dorothy in her early stages.

Trust and hope in God has an amazing, miraculous effect upon negativity! It provides for hope and purpose outside of one's own strength and resources. Dorothy's encounter with God revolutionised her situation, because it was so real and personal and brought with it the realisation of someone who loved her and the promise of, *I will never leave you or forsake you!*[1]

Do you suffer from depression? We need positive encouragement and love, someone who understands – yes, such people do exist!

It is my solemn belief that God's arms never grow tired or weary! Where necessary, He delivers us from all our fears[2] and neither does He condemn or blame us – for so often we can feel guilty and ashamed.[3]

In conclusion, my earnest desire and prayer is to help bring about a caring, understanding empathy with all those who suffer in society today, especially those with mental illness!

Oh, that someone might just place their arms around the person concerned and be Jesus to them!

Will you be such a person?!

"…..assuredly I say to you, inasmuch as you did this to one of the least of these My children, you did it to Me…"
Matthew 25:40

[1] *Hebrews 13:5*

[2] *Psalm 34:4*

[3] *Romans 8:1*

Brian Reddish   November 2015

Books by the Same Author

There is a Balm in Gilead – God's Healing Love, Grace and Compassion
A collection of short stories

Published by Caracal Books

Contact the Author

www.brianreddishbooks.uk
brian@brianreddishbooks.uk

www.ingramcontent.com/pod-product-compliance
Lightning Source LLC
Chambersburg PA
CBHW031944130726
47905CB00002BA/513